THE TROUBLE

WITH MAX

A Teddy and Pip Story

By Lisa Maddock

First published by Cavidae Press
Shakopee, Minnesota 55379

ISBN: 978-0615576954

This book is printed on acid-free paper.
This book is a work of fiction. Places, events, and situations in
this book are purely fictional and any resemblance to actual
persons, living or dead, is coincidental.

Printed in the United States of America.

This one is for all of our beloved pets, past and present, who bring so much joy

PROLOGUE

There it was again, that sound. It was a creepy howling sound that sounded like "boo," or just "oooo." But now there were words too. It sounded like "go away" and "we don't like you." At least that was what it sounded like to Max, a reasonable, regular type of college freshman. Max was not the type to let his imagination go wild on him. He had, in fact, been accused (by a few English teachers over the years) of not having, or using, quite enough imagination. So if what he was hearing sounded like "go away" and "we don't like you," chances were good that that was precisely what was being said.

But who - or *what* - was saying it? That was the big question, wasn't it?

As far as where the sounds were coming from, it was definitely inside the house. And Max was alone in the house; he was sure of that. He had checked every corner already, even in closets and under the bed upstairs. There was no one in that house but him. Him and those guinea pigs. And maybe a... ghost?

No. No way. He did not believe in ghosts.

This job was not going smoothly at all. So far it had been one unexpected thing after the next. And now, on top of everything else, there was a ghost. Possibly. But probably not. Max did not believe in ghosts.

Max was stuck there, in the home of Professor Holmby and his wife, for a very long weekend. From Friday morning to Monday night, to be exact. It was now only Friday night. Technically, it was Saturday morning. Friday had been a long, strange day with little sleep in it, and Saturday was not shaping up to be much better.

Fortunately for his employers, Max was a trustworthy and honest dude. He had been paid one hundred dollars cash to spend three nights and most of four days in this little house in order to watch over the couple's amazingly fussy and spoiled guinea pigs. And a promise was a promise, and a deal was a deal. And since a promise was a promise, he would stay until the bitter end. No matter what.

"Goooooooo awaaaaaaaaaaaay! We dooooooooooon't like youuuuuuuuuuuuuuuuuu!"

Chapter One
A New Assignment

It was Wednesday afternoon, and Amelia and I were having tea. Amelia likes to "have tea" when we have business meetings. I am not a big fan of tea. But if I put enough sugar in it, it isn't so bad. What I do like are the cookies and how Amelia Dearling treats me like a grown-up and a friend even though there is some difference in our ages. My name is Molly Jane Fisher and I am ten years old. Amelia is older, but we do not talk about the specifics. That is just plain good manners and good sense, two things I have a lot of.

The little house was very quiet because it was Teddy and Pip's nap time. If they were awake and knew I was there, it would be noisy for sure. Teddy and Pip are amazing guinea pigs, but more about them later. Amelia and I were at the kitchen table using china cups while eating fancy cookies from a fancy plate. I had my notebook out and a purple pen all ready so I could take notes. After some polite small-talk about the weather and stuff, Amelia set her tea cup down and dabbed at the corners of her mouth with a flowery napkin. I did the same. Then she asked a surprising question of me.

"What do you know about the Nubb boy, Molly?"

I felt the corners of my mouth tug down and my eyes scrunch up. What I knew about Benny Nubb was nothing good. He was a bully, and, too bad for them, he also happened to be Wally and Amelia's next-door neighbor. "Mom says if I don't have anything good to say, I should say nothing," I said, taking a sip of my very sugary tea. "So... I will say nothing."

Amelia's face got worried, and she said, "Oh dear."

"Why?" I set the tea down carefully, hardly spilling any.

"Well, Molly, the reason I have asked you to tea today is because I have some suspicions...."

"About Benny Nubb?" I interrupted. "What did he do?"

Amelia waved her hands around a bit. "As I said, they are suspicions. There is no proof. And I would like to hire you, Molly, to get some proof one way or the other."

I made my eyes squinty and crunched on a cookie. "What do you have suspicion that he did?"

Amelia sipped her tea for a whole minute before she answered me. "Teddy and Pip insist that someone has been prowling about during the night."

"Prowling about?" I gasped.

"Peeking in the windows, tapping on them, making... noises."

I frowned hard. That sounded like exactly the kind of thing Benny Nubb would do. "Do the Nubbs know you have guinea pigs?" I asked, making a note in my notebook with the purple pen.

Amelia shook her head. "We have not spoken with them to any extent at all, so I don't see how they could know. Will you take the job, Molly? Will you try to find out if our neighbor's son is making mischief?"

"You bet I will!"

"Good. Thank you."

"I haven't actually had an interesting case in a while," I said.

Amelia smiled and sipped her tea, then said, "Sometimes that is a blessing. Am I right?"

I shrugged. "I'll need to get Daddy to let me use the video camera for some surveillance. You don't mind if I do that, do you?"

Amelia shook her head.

"And I might need to do a stakeout."

"Whatever you need to do Molly. I trust your detective instincts. And I appreciate this so much. It has gotten to the point where the boys will not sleep downstairs at night. I have been bringing them up to my room to sleep in a portable sleeping area. And that is... well, not so very convenient or private."

"I bet," I said. I had had that exact experience myself, sharing a bedroom with Teddy and Pip.

"Pip does not sleep for very long at any time, and he does tend to burst into song." Amelia smoothed at her hair as I giggled, then smiled. "So, is Detective Molly on the case?"

"Yes I am. At your service! I just need to check with Mom and Dad about some things and then I'll start questioning some people in the neighborhood. Maybe Nora can help me."

"Lovely. Thank you, Molly."

"So, when does Wally get back?" I asked, taking another sip of my tea, which was now cold and thick.

"Not until late Friday night, I'm afraid," Amelia said.

"Don't worry, I'll see what I can find out for you," I said.

She smiled some more. "Shall we move to the living room?"

We left our tea on the table, but brought the cookies and my notebook. Amelia set them on top of a doily on the coffee table and I watched her eyes get confused. She looked around the room, then back at the coffee table. "Well. That is peculiar," she said.

"What is peculiar? Another mystery?"

"I had a little statue on the table here, a figurine of a little girl with an umbrella. It was a gift from my mother and is very special to me. I don't see it anywhere." She turned to me.

I jotted a note in my notebook about that. Maybe we were dealing with not only prowling, but *stealing*, too. I narrowed my eyes about that Benny Nubb. I would get him for this. Nobody scares Teddy and Pip and then steals important things from my best friends and gets away with it!

Amelia stopped frowning about her missing statue. "So tell me about your trip to Disney World, Molly. I hope it was a pleasant experience."

"Disney World was *awesome*," I said. "But I felt so bad about being far away when you and Wally were away, too. I was worried about Teddy and Pip, like, fifty percent of the time."

"Yes, I know. I'm sorry that you had to have worries on your mind when you were in the happiest place on earth." Amelia smiled.

I shrugged. "I didn't worry all the time, just half. I talked to Max a couple times and gave him advice."

"Well, good."

"It sure turned out great, Max staying with Teddy and Pip. It was a miracle, really, how great it all turned out." I still couldn't believe that, and it looked like Amelia couldn't believe it either.

Amelia nodded. "Yes. Something of a miracle." Her smile turned into a slight frown about that.

"Teddy and Pip have actually said good things about Max," I went on. "Compared to how they used to talk about him, it's almost like they actually like him now. Or something."

Amelia said, "Hmm."

We frowned together about that situation then I said, "It turned out the opposite of what I expected. I mean, when they found out that Max was going to stay with them for the weekend, they were really, really upset...."

Chapter Two
Last Thursday

I walked into the kitchen with Tweets on my head to grab a handful of Oreos. But I forgot all about cookies when I heard Wally's voice. He wasn't getting instructions on how to water Mom's plants and take care of our mail. He was saying something to Mom about being away for a while himself. And that was a disaster!

"What's going on, Wally?" I asked as my face frowned-up. I worked at getting Tweets off my head because he was chewing on my hair. He resisted and climbed all over my head. "Where are you going? You can't leave Teddy and Pip! Not now!"

Mom had some hushed words to say to me about that very true statement.

But Wally smiled fondly like he always does and sighed at the same time. He smoothed at his salt-and-peppery hair and shook his head. "I am afraid we have a bit of a situation on our hands, Miss Molly."

"A situation?" I breathed, feeling tense all over. "What is it?"

"Due to a very unfortunate set of circumstances, I am being called up to repay a favor for a dear professor friend who lives in Minnesota." "Minnesota?" I gasped. Minnesota was very far away. Much too far from New Jersey where we lived. I didn't know exactly how far it was, but it felt like a million miles away.

"He will be going into the hospital for a procedure on Saturday morning. Of course, he will be quite unable to finish the semester where he teaches Economics while he recovers. He is also scheduled to do a seminar for a group of businessmen in town on Saturday afternoon. He has asked me to step in and I have agreed."

Mom, not realizing, as usual, that this was a disaster, said, "It is so kind of you to fill in for your friend, Wally. Who will cover classes for you while you are away?"

"I have a trustworthy colleague and my teaching assistant ready to step in."

"Why can't *that* person go to Minnesota?" I asked. "The trustworthy one? Then you can stay here." It made perfect sense to me, but neither grown-up even considered it for a second.

Mom actually gave me one of her looks, then said, "Don't worry, we'll figure something out," to Wally.

I crossed my arms as Tweets flew up to the ceiling fan, taking a few of my hairs with him. Ouch. "How are we going to figure it out?" I asked, rubbing my head. My mom totally does not understand Teddy and Pip. I looked at Wally.

"It is indeed bad timing," he sighed, which was an understatement if ever there was one.

"Could Amelia come home early?" I asked, but Wally's head was shaking before I finished the sentence. "The earliest she can be back is Monday evening, I am afraid."

I groaned. "That's when we're coming back! Well, that does it. We'll just have to cancel our trip." My eyes moved to the table full of Disney plans, brochures, tickets, and swimming stuff to pack and I felt a twist of sorry for myself.

"You will do no such thing," Wally said with a warm smile as Mom shook her head very firmly about that selfless but necessary idea. "I do appreciate the gesture, Miss Molly, but you have been looking forward to this vacation for so very long, and it is, I assume, all paid for?"

I shrugged and looked at Mom, who was nodding, firmly. Then Mom's eyes went to the ceiling fan then back to mine. Mom and I have communication that does not need to be said out loud sometimes. She was saying: *that bird had better not poop on the kitchen table*, and also wanting me to get Tweets out of the kitchen. Which was very off the subject.

"Who is going to take care of Tweets?!" I asked, as that extra problem popped into my head. "You were going to feed him every day and check his water, Wally!"

"Ah, yes," Wally said, smoothing at his mustache. "There is also that. I do apologize, my friend."

"Nora is going out of town, too!" I added, starting to feel hysteria. "There is no one to turn to! This is a disaster! What are we going to do?"

Wally chuckled warmly about it being a disaster. He does that - chuckles warmly - about just about everything. Even disasters, apparently. "Surely, if we put our brilliant set of heads together, we can come up with a trustworthy and available individual who can care for Teddy and Pip for a few days, and also Mr. Tweets."

"Seriously? Like who?"

Mom sighed, her eyes focusing and squinting up at Tweets again instead of urgent problem-solving. "Molly?"

I climbed up on the table and stuck a finger under Tweets' belly until he climbed up, then carried him back down, hardly messing up or knocking anything over at all.

"I believe the best place for him is *upstairs* when we have company," Mom said, pointing to a poop that had ended up on the top plane ticket, which unfortunately had the name Jane Fisher on it.

"Wally isn't company," I pointed out.

Wally chuckled and agreed. "I am more like family. Definitely a friend," he said, then added that we should never worry or fuss on his behalf. But we always do.

"Come on Tweets. You have just put yourself in the dog house," I said, letting him climb back up onto my head and wiping the poop off of Mom's plane ticket. "You have to go upstairs, even though Wally is not company."

When I got back to the kitchen, the grown-ups were sitting at the table, sipping coffee and looking like their brains were smoking from deep thoughts. "I know!" Mom said suddenly. "My nephew Max! He is always and forever needing cash, and I can't imagine why he would be unavailable at this point with his finals going on."

Mom smiled about her great idea, but my mouth dropped open and I stood frozen like a popsicle.

"Hmm," Wally said.

"He is a freshman at the university. A good, solid young man. Dan and I trust him with Molly," Mom added, as if that had anything to do with Max being trusted with the guinea pigs. Then Mom stood up and said, "I'll call him right away."

"Stop!" I said, unfreezing, my voice sounding very serious. "You can't ask Max to watch Teddy and Pip! That is a terrible idea! No offense," I added because Mom was looking squinty-eyed at me.

"Molly, for goodness sake, why not?" Mom put her hands on her hips.

"Because they don't like Max," I said quietly. "They don't trust him."

This information made Mom do an exasperated sound, pause in her phone call quest, and begin to set things out for making dinner. "Those guinea pigs have never met Max," she said. "I'm sorry, but that is not a good reason."

"No, they haven't, but...."

"It is not actually necessary for the boys to meet someone before forming a strong opinion," Wally said with a gentle voice. "Do they... have a strong opinion about Max, Miss Molly?"

I nodded slowly but surely and Wally's eyebrows went up.

Mom did a huff. She was not liking that her plan was being rejected. "Well, we don't have another option, do we? It seems to me that you two need to find a way to convince those opinionated guinea pigs that their strong opinion of Max is faulty. Or else they will just plain have to deal with him being around in spite of their strong opinions."

Chapter Three
Introducing Max

Max had plenty of troubles. He way too busy with finals, much too broke, always hungry, and, worst of all, oh so crazy about a girl. Plenty of troubles for one nineteen-year-old to handle all at once. Anything more and he would pretty much be toast.

Studying Economics while lying on the sagging couch turned into napping before long. The Economics book lay across his chest and a yellow line zig-zagged across page 135. His highlighter had long since slid to the floor.

He was awakened from a dream about flying and... Sophie... by the ringing of his cell phone. Actually, the pounding out of a regrettably loud Sousa march. Max sat up too quickly, dropped his text book to the floor, banged his knee against the coffee table, and grappled for the phone.

"Arrrgh, *ouch*...."

"Max, is that you? It's Aunt Jane."

"Oh, yeah, hey, Aunt Jane. What's up?" Max rubbed his knee as he slumped back onto the couch.

"I didn't wake you, did I?" Aunt Jane sounded surprised or disapproving about that possibility. Apparently she had no memory of the exhausting nature of college.

"Asleep? Me? No. It's like... it's the afternoon... or something. Isn't it?" Max looked around for a timepiece, found none and shrugged. "What's up? Is everything all right?"

"Well, yes, of course. In general," Jane said with a sigh. "We're leaving for Florida in the morning, you know."

"Oh, right. You guys need a ride to the airport at, like, the crack of dawn." Max grimaced about that promise he had made a week ago – before he knew it was so early in the morning.

"Yes. We need to leave the house at 5:30, I'm afraid. But I'm actually calling now for a different additional favor, Max."

Max felt himself tighten up. A different additional favor? A favor in addition to getting up at five o'clock in the morning the day of a big test? He loved Aunt Jane and her family. They were the best and always there for him, but....

The truth was, or seemed to be, that he simply had no time or energy for favor-doing, not at this point in time. He was totaled out. His ten-year-old cousin Molly was a great kid, kind of a super-smart, mini-adult type of kid. She was easy to hang out with. But kid-sitting with Molly would mean he'd miss out on study time tonight. And besides, Molly always seemed to get him into bizarro situations. Bizarro situations were just plain not welcome on the agenda during finals week.

But then again, on the other hand or side of the coin, he would be likely to get a free pizza and some quick cash out of the deal. Cash which would buy more pizza - which always helped a lot with the studying. Max rubbed his eyes with his free hand, then thinking much more about pizza than his Econ final, heard himself ask. "What else can I do?"

"Well, let me tell you about it," Jane said, sounding suddenly hesitant, possibly (confusingly) apologetic about asking him to watch Molly tonight, "before you say you can do it."

"Uh huh...." Max nodded slowly.

"Friends of ours, Wally and Amelia, who just moved to a house down our street - Wally teaches Economics at Princeton...."

"Princeton, huh?" Max's eyes flicked guiltily toward the Econ text book which was in a rather undignified heap on the floor. He leaned down to pick it up then smoothed a crumpled page.

"They have guinea pigs," Jane was continuing.

"Oh, sure, the guinea pig people. Yeah, yeah, yeah, I heard about those guys from Molly." Max felt himself relax a bit. The additional favor had something to do with feeding someone's little pets. He could do that, no sweat. That was even easier than sitting with Molly.

"Wally and Amelia used to live in our garage apartment."

"Yep. I remember." Max suppressed a yawn and flopped back down on the couch.

"It is rare that it happens, but when they have to both be away, they ask Molly to take care of the, uh, pets for them."

"But you guys are going to see Mickey. Leaving the house at 5:30 a.m. I get it. I'll do it, no problem."

Jane went on, "It just so happens that Amelia is away on a book tour right now and Wally has an out-of-town emergency that will take him away until the end of next week."

"So it's time for the B squad, I get it. Aunt Jane, if they need someone to feed their little pets, I can totally do that. No big deal. Just give me an address."

"No big deal," Jane echoed. "Ah, yes, well...." She cleared her throat a little then said. "They are rather particular about these guinea pigs and their care."

"Okay. Got it. Have 'em write it all down. I'll take care of it. You need me to feed that parakeet of Molly's, too?"

"Yes, if you would." Jane hesitated, then said, "Wally would like someone to actually stay with them, the guinea pigs, as much of Friday, the weekend, and Monday as possible. At their house."

Max didn't say anything for a little while. He was pondering the situation, mainly wondering what the catch could be. He had very little problem with leaving his crowded, noisy, stale-smelling, messy dorm room for a whole weekend to be in a little house all by himself. Ever since his roommate broke up with that last girlfriend, the place had definitely taken a bad turn as far as neatness. The professor's house, without a doubt, would be quiet and clean. They would probably give him food too. Food and sleep were rather important to Max. And quiet would be, like, awesome for studying.

"Wally is willing to pay one hundred dollars," Jane went on, as if Max needed even more convincing.

"Did you say *one hundred dollars*? Whoa! Aunt Jane, you had me at hello. When do I show up?"

"Why don't you join us for dinner tonight? I'll have Wally stop by so you can meet and perhaps discuss Economics. Your test is tomorrow, am I right?"

"What's for dinner?" Max interrupted.

"Fried chicken, potatoes, vegetables...."

"All over it, Aunt Jane. I am there."

"After dinner, Wally can take you down the street to his house and introduce you to the animals. If you'd like, you can spend the night in our guest room."

"This is starting to be, like, perfect," Max said with a contented sigh. "Aunt Jane? Could I, uh, bring over some laundry? It is uncool to ask? The laundry machines here at my dorm are toast right now." Max knew from past experience that Jane, like his own mother, would not be able to leave a pile of dirty laundry sitting in her laundry room. She would begin to process it through without much thought or effort at all, and clothes would appear all nice and fresh, folded and smooth by morning. Moms were awesome like that, even when they weren't your own.

Max left a brief note for his roommate, Alex, in case the dude happened to notice that he wasn't around. Then he packed up all of his clothes, dirty and clean (because who could really tell one from the other in a situation like his?) and headed for his car to spend a few quiet, clean, peaceful nights away from the dorm.

Chapter Four
Breaking the News

Wally had made a point of giving Teddy and Pip extra veggies, extra attention, and extra reading Thursday night. He finished a solid chapter of the book before setting it down. Then he took a deep breath and broke the news. "A dear friend of mine from Minnesota, whose name is Eli...."

"We would like to hear more Potter, not about that stuff," Teddy said, his mouth full of lettuce. *"We do not know of this person or of that place. It is not so very interesting or exciting so far. Ho hum."*

Pip nodded in agreement. *"WE WOULD LIKE TO HEAR MORE OF THE POTTER STORY! DO NOT TAKE UP OUR TIME WITH STORIES OF PEOPLE WE DO NOT KNOW, WALLY! DO NOT MAKE US MAD, OKAY?"*

"Boys, I am not merely telling stories to entertain you this evening. I am bringing up my friend Eli because I need to explain why I need to be away for a while."

"Wally! You cannot be away at this time!" Teddy squeaked.

"OBJECTION!" Pip squealed in his high, squeaky voice. *"AWAY IS NO GOOD!"*

"Boys, I am sorry to do this to you. Please believe that I truly am. But I must come to the aid of my friend. He is in great need of my help and there is simply no one else he can turn to," Wally continued, over increasing protests. "Eli has helped me a great deal in the past, and now he needs me to teach his Economics classes for a couple of weeks."

"Our friend Wally has sleepy kids to teach Economics to already at his Princeton," Teddy said. *"So, the end!"*

"THE END!" Pip echoed.

"Boys, I promised Eli that if he ever was in need, I would be there for him. And a promise is a promise, and a deal is a deal. This is an important lesson for you to learn as well."

"The lesson to learn is that this person called Eli needs to get his help from a person who is not our best friend Wally," Teddy said. *"Amelia is away and we need a friend to feed us and care for all of our important needs. You cannot leave us all alone for days and days and weeks and...."*

"Theodore, of course I would never ever leave you alone like that. Surely you know that by now."

"But you did leave us once for a long time, and more time than that, and it was the worst of times! Mom Jane put us in a bucket, Wally! Remember that time? That is unreasonable! Surely there are people in that place called Mini Soda who are not bad and can help your friend, who is not our friend. The end. Now we can read Potter! Yippee!"

"*CASE CLOSED!*"

"Sometimes in life, we need to make certain sacrifices in order to help out our fellow man," Wally plowed ahead.

"*WE ARE NOT FELLOW MEN AND WE OBJECT!*" Pip screamed. "*YOU NEED TO GIVE UP, WALLY. WE WIN! CASE DISMISSED! POTTER TIME!*"

Wally sighed. "I am truly sorry that this emergency has come up at such an inconvenient time - and I do know how difficult it is for you to deal with a change in your routine."

"*We will only let a best friend care for us, and that means only just Wally, Amelia, Molly Jane or Dad,*" Teddy said loudly so he could be heard over Pip's further dismissal of the case. "*No others will do. Anyone else is fired or dismissed. If all best friends are the thing of away, then Wally cannot leave us so he will stay and we will have much fun together, just like we planned, until Amelia comes home. I will tell you what, Wally friend, you can go help that Mini Soda person who has no other friends when Amelia comes home. That is my final offer. The end!*"

"Max, who is Molly's trusted cousin, will be stopping by this evening to meet you and to hear instructions for taking care of you," Wally said, "so please show him the courtesy that you would like to be shown yourself if the shoe was on the other foot, so to speak...."

"*MAX?! DID YOU SAY MAX?!*" Pip shrieked. "*MAX CANNOT COME HERE! HE IS NO GOOD, WALLY! PLUS ALSO, WE DO NOT WEAR SHOES*"

ON EITHER OF OUR FEET! DO NOT MAKE US MAD! YOU ARE MAKING US MAD!" Pip stood up against the walkway railing to show his paws. *"WE ARE NOT LIKING THAT YOU WOULD LET MAX BE IN OUR PERFECT HOME WITH HIS SMELLY FEET! WHAT IS WRONG WITH YOU WALLY?!"*

"Now, Pippen, is that a kind thing to say?"

Teddy defended Pip in a conversational tone, *"It is actually a true thing to say, Wally friend. You should not be letting that no-good Max come to our perfect home where he will be unkind to guinea pigs and say wrong things and not feed us and do it all wrong. You know better than that. We are disappointed."* Teddy shook his head back and forth.

"Good heavens, Theodore! How could you possibly have such a negative opinion of Molly's cousin, whom you have never even met?"

"WE KNOW!" Pip said darkly. *"YOU MUST TRUST THAT WE KNOW GOOD PEOPLE AND NOT GOOD PEOPLE! MAX IS NO GOOD - HE IS THE WORST OF ALL TIMES!"*

"He will not feed us," Teddy said, his tone a little less firm than before. *"He will never give us what we need, Wally. We will be starving if that Max comes here for days and days and does not feed us!"*

"Why in heaven's name would Max, or anyone else who has been asked to care for you, not feed you?" Wally asked reasonably. "I cannot think of a single person who would deny you your meals. More than likely, a caregiver would be completely accommodating and your lives would be quite pleasant for the days when I am gone. Why would Max be the one exception to that rule?"

"*He will do it all wrong,*" Teddy said quietly. "*It will be the worst of times back again. Like those days when there was no Wally and no Amelia.*"

"*WE CANNOT DO THAT THING AGAIN WITH NO MOLLY JANE TO SAVE OUR DAY! OBJECTION! OBJECTION! OBJECTION!*" Pip ran shrieking up and down the ramp.

"Boys, it could never and will never be like those days again! I assure you that I will be checking in at least once a day and speaking with Max, and asking him to put you on the phone so I can hear for myself that you are fine," Wally promised. "Please, for me, and for the sake of all of us, I need your cooperation."

Pip whispered, "*COOPERATION IS THE OPPOSITE OF BEST OF TIMES. WALLY IS ON THE THIN ICE.*"

"I am sorry boys, but this is the way it is going to be, whether you agree or not. I need to leave in the morning and Max will be staying with you. I recommend that you improve your attitude towards him, but that is up to you, of course. It will be a much more pleasant weekend if you give him a chance."

Chapter Five
The Gig

"Aunt Jane, this is awesome!" Max shoveled a big spoonful of mashed potatoes into his mouth. "Mmmm mmmm! I was starving!"

"Good heavens, Max, don't you have some sort of a meal plan at school?" Mom fussed, setting the platter of chicken right in front of the eating machine.

"Oh sure, yeah, but... I mean there's eating, and then there's *eating!*" Max said with his mouth full.

"Well, it is always a pleasure having you at the dinner table. Clearly, no one appreciates my cooking more than you."

I frowned about that comment. "I appreciate your cooking," I mumbled, moving my potatoes around. "I just like spaghetti better."

"Well, show your appreciation by eating everything on your plate," Mom said. She always says stuff like that to make me feel guilty when I don't love her dinners. She raised her eyebrows up at me.

"So, Max," I said, picking up a kernel of corn with my fork and examining it carefully. It looked a little less yellow than it should be. "You love guinea pigs, right?"

Max shrugged and nodded, still chewing.

"I mean *love*. You have to totally *LOVE* them if you are going to watch Teddy and Pip," I said loudly, frowning at him intensely. "Not just the same as you love food or your car... but like you love your *mom!*"

Max stared with his mouth open a bit. "I don't know, Mol. Love is a pretty strong word. And, I mean, I haven't exactly hung with guinea pigs too much. Ya know? Love takes time, and stuff."

"Well, then, you have to *act* like you love them. You have to treat them like they are really special, important little people. If you don't feel real love, then you have to convince them that you do. It is *very* important!"

Max flicked his eyes to my mom, then my dad. They both smiled and shrugged a little. "O... kay. Little people. Love. If I don't feel it, fake it. Gotcha."

"They are *very* sensitive about everything. You have to watch what you say around them. And don't forget to do everything that Wally tells you to do. Everything. Even if it seems like a lot!"

Max was frowning now. "I'll do whatever the professor says, Mol. He's paying me good money to take care of his... little dudes. Why would I want to blow it? It's awesome cash, and should be real easy. It's not like they're kids or anything. They don't have to do homework or brush their teeth, right? I'm sure they are a lot less trouble than, for example, *you*. They just sit around or whatever and eat. Right?" Max looked around at all of us.

"Be sure that you are really nice to them and totally respectful. Their names are Teddy and Pip. They're boys, not girls. Teddy is the bigger one. They are really smart and they don't like just *anyone*."

Max nodded as he piled more food onto his plate. "They'll like me. I'm going to be my most likable. Don't worry, Mol. What about your bird? How about if I bring him over so I can, like, feed him and watch over all of them at once?"

"No!" I hollered that and got some serious looks from my parents. "It's a bad idea," I said a lot more quietly. "Just don't. Sorry Max, but you'll have to come over here to feed Tweets. You need to trust me on this." I looked at Mom who gave a little head-shake.

Max, who was looking up at that moment to reach for even more food, noticed. "Okay. What's going on here? What are you ladies - and gentleman - not telling me about this gig?"

"Molly is being overly protective, Max," Mom said, handing him the bowl of potatoes. "That's all."

"I'll be good to them," Max said. "Honest. I like animals. Gee whiz! What do you think I am, a monster?"

"You might have to read to them." I tried my hardest to sound casual. "They especially like Charles Dickens. But right now I think Wally is reading *Harry Potter* to them. Don't say Voldemort out loud. They don't like that."

Max stopped eating again and stared, his spoon halfway to his mouth. "Say that again, Mol?"

"*A Tale of Two Cities* and *Harry Potter*," I said impatiently. "They like to hear it. They especially like Charles Dickens."

"Uh...." Max set his spoon down. "That's the dude who wrote *A Christmas Carol*, right? That was, like, a Muppet movie?"

Mom and Dad smiled at him encouragingly but I felt a big knot tightening up in my insides. This was trouble.

"I'm sure Wally will let you know the... particulars," Mom said, giving me one of her warning looks because she thought I was about to blow the whole deal. "Perhaps they are not reading any Dickens just now."

Max laughed, but no one joined him so he stopped.

"They like their schedules," I said. "Whatever it is, you have to do it or they'll be upset."

"Okay Mol, I'll follow the schedules," Max said. "Promise." He was looking a bit uneasy now and I decided to back off because maybe I was blowing the whole deal. The clock was ticking on us and Max was our last hope.

Daddy saved the day, or at least the moment, by changing the subject to baseball. Some team was playing some other team and yawn, yawn, yawn.

I looked at Mom who shook her head warningly at me. But, I mean, gee whiz! I had to tell him. I had to let him know what he was up against. Didn't I? It was going to be a disaster anyway, but at least I could make it a little less of one.

"Molly and I will clear the table now," Mom announced, pushing her chair back. "I'll have some dessert ready in a few minutes."

"Awesome!" Max said with a happy smile. "This is great. I'm thinking I should just totally move in here with you guys next quarter."

"Molly," Mom said, keeping her voice whispery as I scraped gunky food off of plates and into the garbage, "we need to be careful about what kind of information we give Max about those guinea pigs. Wally and Amelia do not want any more people to know about the... talking thing." She cleared her throat, then started to cut the brownies into squares.

"I know. But I am really worried about them. They already think they don't like Max so they'll be really miserable."

"Miserable is a strong word," Mom said, handing me a stack of small plates with napkins and forks on top. "They might miss familiar people but they will be fine."

I wanted to believe her, but "Mom Jane" was not the best one to know about how Teddy and Pip would act, feel, or be. I knew. They would be miserable.

"Wally is coming over shortly to talk to Max, and probably help him out with some Economics studying for a while. Then the two of them will head over to the house. I bet Wally will let you scoot over to his house while he's here with Max so you can have some time with... them. What do you think of that?"

Chapter Six
Max Isn't So Bad, Guys!

I made my way down the street to Teddy and Pip's house with Daddy, who was jingling the keys and listening to that baseball game through ear phones. I had a plastic baggie of parsley in my hands and was thinking hard about what to say. I gave Benny Nubb a frowning look as he passed us on his bike and that icky boy stuck his tongue out at me.

Daddy did a quick check all around to be sure the house was safe and secure for me, because that's what dads do. It was really quick because my dad is allergic to the fur of animals and always has to come and go fast so he doesn't get a runny or stuffy nose. "All clear, kiddo! Have a nice visit!" He told me to lock back up and that he'd be back to fetch me in a little bit.

I shook the plastic bag so the guys would know I was there and it worked like a charm.

"*Molly Jane!*" Teddy squealed. "*Molly Jane is here for us! Try to find me, Molly Jane! I am hiding from you! Tee hee!*"

"COME AND FIND US IN OUR MAZE! TEE HEE! BEST OF TIMES IS HIDING FROM BEST FRIENDS!"

"Molly Jane, after we do hide-and-seek we can play Harry Potter! You will be He-Who-Must-Not-Be-Named!"

"DON'T SAY THE NAME!" Pip hollered.

Playing "Harry Potter" is their newest thing. I get to be Voldemort every time. Teddy is Harry and Pip is... Harry. What can I say? They run away from me squealing and shoot curses at me. That is how it's done, and I don't argue because Teddy and Pip are the real bosses – of everything.

Teddy and Pip's new house is really cool. I mean, it's perfectly perfect for them. I was so sad when Wally and Amelia told us they were moving out of the garage apartment, but then they said they were only moving down the street, less than one block away. So I was relieved and happy, but also shocked down to my socks to find out that they were moving into the haunted house next door to the Nubbs. But that's what they did.

Wally, who is an amazing wood-worker, fixed it all up to be cute, cozy, and guinea pig-friendly. All around the main level of the house is a walkway with a clear plastic ledge for the guinea pigs. The ledge is just high enough for safety, but low enough for Teddy and Pip to peek over the top as they walk around and around from room to room, exploring, playing hide and seek, and getting lots of exercise. There are no doors on the rooms downstairs so they can come and go with no troubles.

In the office, which is just off of the cozy living room, is where their enormous two-story house sits. It takes up most of the room and is filled with cozy cushions and beds, places to hide or nap, and, of course, there is a TV set.

"I give up. Where are you guys? I have some yummy parsley. I'll start eating it myself if you aren't out here in ten seconds...." I would never eat parsley, of course. Blech. But saying it worked, as far as getting them to come out of hiding.

"Don't eat it, Molly Jane! Parsley is no good for humans!" Teddy squealed. *"Parsley is only made for guinea pigs like us!"*

I handed them each a piece and they dropped to all fours and started to slurp it up like spaghetti. "Guys? I need to talk to you about the weekend."

"There is no need for that talk," Teddy informed me. *"We have decided that Wally will stay and Max is fired. The end. Or else Molly Jane will stay with us."*

I stroked his head. "I'm sorry, honey. But I can't. I am going to Florida with Mom and Dad."

"Molly Jane, Florida is not the place to go. It is a bad place full of monsters and..." Teddy hesitated before finishing, *"... oranges. Bad oranges, not good ones."*

"MOM JANE IS NO GOOD!" Pip added. *"SHE PUT US IN A BUCKET, CALLED US MONSTERS! FLORIDA IS NO GOOD! WORST OF TIMES IS MOLLY JANE IN FLORIDA WHEN WALLY IS IN NO-GOOD MINNESOTA AND AMELIA IS... WHERE IS AMELIA?!"*

"This is what we call bad timing," I said, petting Pip. "I wish I could be the one to take care of you but...."

"There is a thing called cancel. You can cancel this Florida thing-a-ma-thing. Florida is not good for Molly Jane anyway," Teddy said. *"There are alligators and other monsters there. Okay, Molly Jane? Please?"*

"WORST OF TIMES!" Pip said, giving my hand a lick. *"NOW I REMEMBER IT! AMELIA IS FAR AWAY IN THE PLACE OF OREGON! WORST OF TIMES IS BEST FRIENDS ALL OVER THE WHOLE WIDE WORLD!"*

I took a deep breath. "My cousin Max is a good guy. He can be a good friend if you give him a chance. Will you give him a chance? For me?"

"We don't like him," Teddy said quietly. *"Max is no good and you cannot talk us out of it."*

"MAX... IS... NO... GOOD!" Pip spoke firmly and loudly.

"We do not trust him. He will not do good things. He will not feed us or do the right things. We know this." Teddy's soft dark eyes were making my insides melt into a puddle of sadness.

"Yes, of course he will! I promise you he will. I have already talked to him and I will talk to him some more to be sure of that."

Teddy and Pip continued to shake their heads.

"Max helped us out when Amelia and Wally were missing last summer, remember? He helped me to get the video onto the TV so we could solve the mystery."

"*Nice try, Molly Jane, but no dice.*"

"*MAX IS FIRED!*"

"Look, guys, you know I totally, totally love you. You have to know that I would not be okay with *anyone* taking care of you unless I believed that person was really good. Does that make sense? You can trust me. And you can certainly trust Wally. Would he ever ask Max to come here if he thought he wouldn't take good care of you?"

"*Max is not our friend,*" Teddy said. "*We love Molly Jane, Wally, and Amelia. Mom Jane is no good.*"

"*MAX IS NO GOOD!*" Pip suddenly changed his tone and sounded happy. "*BUT DAD DAN CAN COME! HE IS A FRIEND WHO BROUGHT CHRISTMAS ONE DAY SOME TIME AGO!*"

"Well, honey, Daddy is going to Florida with me...."

"*FLORIDA IS NO GOOD! WHY DOES THERE HAVE TO BE THAT PLACE?!*" Pip squealed. "*IT IS FULL OF ALLIGATOR MONSTERS!*"

"I'm sorry, you guys. I hoped I could make you feel better, but I don't think I did. I wish there was something else I could do or say. I'll send you a postcard. Would you like that? Maybe Max could read it to you?"

"*We do not think Max would do that.*" Teddy sounded sad and it broke my puddly heart into pieces. "*We know he won't. He would not read us the postcard, Molly Jane. He would keep it from us like Bad Barbara.*"

There was no time to say anything that might help the situation. The door opened and Wally stepped in with Max behind him. And Teddy and Pip ran as fast as their little legs would carry them toward their house.

"Molly, my friend, your father is waiting for you on the front step," Wally said, reaching his hand out to give me a goodbye shake. "Have a good time on your trip."

"You too, I guess. I wish you didn't have to go," I said.

"As do I. It is most unfortunate."

"They'll be okay, right?"

Wally nodded, though he didn't seem as sure as I wanted him to seem.

"See you later, Mol," Max called from the kitchen. "I'll be back after I learn the ropes here. Maybe we can grab a snack and watch some TV.... Scratch that. 'Cuz I'll be studying for my test, of course." He glanced at Wally, who smiled.

Chapter Seven
Orientation

Max ran his hand along the guinea pig walkway and peeked inside. "Hey - there's, like, a carrot in here," he said, holding it up for Wally to see.

Wally took it from him and smiled. "This is the boys' specially made walking area, Max. It is actually quite unusual to find food lying about anywhere. Teddy and Pip are more likely to eat it." He chuckled.

"I can respect that," Max said.

"They don't tend to be untidy, generally. So I don't expect you to do any sort of cleaning while you are here. But if you do happen to spy some food discarded along this walkway, could you pop it into the trash?"

"Sure thing. No sweat. Did you build this racetrack for them?" Max asked, continuing to wander from room to room. "I've never heard of anything like this. It's like – a model train without tracks, like, all around the house."

"Yes, I did indeed. These are very special guinea pigs. They are family to us. It is good for them to have their exercise and this walkway gives them independence to do it safely when they get the urge. They can get themselves into a bit of trouble if allowed to roam about on the ground."

"Yeah, I bet."

Wally excused himself to answer a phone call in the kitchen, leaving Max alone in the living room. It was very quiet, very neat, and very seeming to have no guinea pigs in it. "Hello?" he called. "Guinea pigs? Dudes? You in there?"

When Wally returned to the living room, Max said, "Thanks for the study help back there. I like money and all that, but the class is just kind of boring... except it's actually kind of interesting the way *you* tell it." Max cringed. "If you were my teacher, I'd be getting an A plus or something even better."

Wally smiled. "Why thank you, Max. That is indeed a compliment. Speaking of money...."

"Oh, you don't have to... I wasn't trying to...." Max felt his ears turning a little bit red with embarrassment. "I wasn't hinting at you about giving me money."

Wally pulled five twenty-dollar bills out of his wallet and handed them firmly to him. "This is our agreed-upon fee. You are doing Amelia and me a great service. We thank you in advance."

Max shoved the money into his pocket, mumbling, "No big deal. Piece of cake."

"Hmm," Wally said with a slight twinkle in his eye. "That remains to be seen, does it not?"

Teddy and Pip remained still and silent in the darkest, most unreachable corner of their house, listening intently to everything that was being said.

"The boys are named Teddy and Pip, short for Theodore Hamilton the Third and Pippen. Teddy has a black face and a white and tan body. Our Pip has a white body and black and brown patches over his eyes. He is definitely our more sassy and spunky fellow. I am hopeful that they will make an appearance soon so you can recognize them on sight. If not, I will show you a photo or two."

Max shrugged and nodded.

"If you happen to see guinea pigs not meeting these descriptions, they are not ours. Please return them to their owners."

Max stared.

"That was a joke."

"Oh! Ha!" Max attempted a laugh, but it didn't actually seem funny to him that there could be guinea pigs running around the place that didn't belong there. "They can't, like, get out of there, can they? Fall or get loose or – anything? And, like, other guinea pigs can't really get in, right?"

Wally smiled. "No, of course not. As you have already seen, the raised walkway, which is completely safe and secure, connects back to their spacious home." Wally walked to the office and stood in front of the living quarters. "I have ensured that the boys are completely safe and secure while in their walkway."

Max gave a low whistle. "Well, good job. I mean, this is something. This guinea pig place is bigger than my dorm room. And cleaner."

Wally chuckled. "Since I see no sign of them, I am assuming that the boys are going to be anti-social with you for the time being. Trust me when I say that they will make their noisy appearance at meal times. Place their vegetables in this area and they will come running, guaranteed."

"When do they want to eat?" Max asked, peering into the doll-house-like home.

"*Want* to? Well, that would be almost constantly. When we actually feed them is first thing in the morning, between 7:00 and 8:00 generally, and at dinner time; somewhere between 4:30 and 6:00 is just fine." Wally discussed the amounts of guinea pig pellets versus hay and fresh vegetables and fruit. But he had actually measured it all out and carefully arranged things on the kitchen counter and in the refrigerator. He had even marked each package with the day and meal.

"This is pretty brainless for me. I mean, you did everything so all I have to do is be, like, a waiter," Max said. "I feel a little bad taking so much cash just for this."

"It is important for the boys to have someone around. It would make them very uneasy indeed to be alone for any amount of time. Your being here will put them at ease."

Max nodded about that.

"It would make them very uneasy, of course, to miss their meals."

"I can respect that. Missing meals is just not cool. Don't worry, Professor."

Wally smiled and nodded, satisfied. "That is the most important thing."

"Got it."

Wally looked thoughtful for a moment. "The neighbor next door may approach you about various things if you are outside. Please tell him it is not necessary to mow my lawn for me." Wally shook his head and sighed about the neighbor.

"Gotcha," Max said.

"Now, as for your meals, the refrigerator is stocked with sandwich ingredients and the freezer with frozen pizzas. In addition, I have left cash for you to order in."

"Professor, this is awesome! You thought of everything," Max murmured. "Thanks!"

"Did I? I feel that I am giving scattered information and am leaving things out."

"Nah, we're cool. Except... where do you want me to sleep?"

"Ah! An important question indeed! The only room with a door down here is our guest room." The professor approached a closed door behind the guinea pigs' walkway. To Max's surprise, he fiddled with something underneath then lifted up a whole section of the walkway in front of the bedroom door. "This hinge creates easier access to the guest room for visiting relatives," Wally said. "But if you do not mind, could I ask you to leave the walkway in place and simply duck under in order to enter the room? Lifting this section does limit the boys' access to the kitchen."

"Sure, no problem," Max said, watching as the professor pulled the raised section back into place and secured it tightly from underneath. "I can duck. Don't want to limit anything." He ducked under and stepped into the bedroom and the professor followed.

"I have freshened up the room for you with clean sheets. There is a bathroom with a shower right next door and I have provided fresh towels." Wally was quiet for a few seconds. "It is a bit... frilly, I know, and I apologize for that." The two males stood regarding the frilly bedroom in silence.

Max cleared his throat. "Aw, don't give it a thought. It's totally fine, Professor. The cleanness is, like, refreshing for me." He gestured at the lacy curtains. "I can handle a little frill. I'll, like, have my eyes closed most of them time in here, anyway, right?"

Wally smiled, nodded agreement, ducked under the ramp, and moved on to the living room. "This room, I must point out, contains some delicate figurines and other important things to Amelia."

"Got it, Professor. I need to watch out for the expensive knick-knacks. My mom has a bunch of that stuff too. I'll keep the place shipshape for you, don't worry."

"Shipshape is not necessary, Max. All we ask is that the house looks like it does now when Amelia returns on Monday evening."

"Okey dokey. So if I'm taking the guest room, where do you sleep, Professor? I don't see any other bedroom around here."

"The staircase off of the kitchen leads to Amelia's and my room – which you should not need to visit for any reason. The guinea pigs are unable to go up there. It is our one bit of privacy in this house."

"You mean you don't have, like, a little elevator they can hop into to go upstairs?"

Wally chuckled about that, then said, "Indeed, no."

"Professor, just wondering on this one - and you can say no if you think it's a bad idea - would it be at all possibly all right for me to have... a certain person... over here? Just one person for a little while? Not a messy *dude* or anything who would wreck the artifacts, but like a female. Maybe Saturday. Maybe. If she says she can come over."

"If you are talking about entertaining a young lady, feel free. I trust that you will behave with complete appropriateness."

Max considered that for a moment then nodded. "I do. I mean, I will. I wanted to lay the cards on the table with you and be above-board and all."

"I appreciate that, Max. Feel free to entertain the young lady if she agrees to it. Large parties, however, would be frowned upon, of course." Wally smiled to soften that message.

"Dude - I mean, Professor - I would never. Ever. I mean, I bet those guinea pigs of yours would totally rat me out if I had a big party anyway."

Wally smiled. "Indeed they would, Max."

Chapter Eight
Friday Morning

"Okay. So... here's your grub, little vegetarian-type dudes!" Max called as he set dishes of lettuce, parsley, carrots, and broccoli in front of the guinea pigs' house. "I gave you, like, a ton of hay. Okay? And I put those little pellet thingies in that other dish too and made sure there's lots of water." He craned his neck around, trying to catch a glimpse of them. No guinea pigs came running. "Um, so, it says here on this list of instructions that you get to watch TV in the morning. SpongeBob. So... do you dudes want me to turn that on for you?" Max scratched his head. "The professor didn't say exactly how that... works. And also, I guess you're reading a book called... well, I forget. It's here somewhere, though. Can we do that later? Maybe we can skip it and watch TV together later. Would that be okay? You guys don't actually *like* listening to some dude reading books at you, do you?"

There was no response, no sound, no rustle of any kind.

"Well, I have to go take my Econ test now." Max looked uneasily at the large living area. All was quiet, and no furry bodies appeared to eat the food he had set out. They were supposed to come out. The professor said they for sure would come out for food.

Max hesitated a few moments more, wondering what he should do, if anything, to improve the situation. What if they didn't eat all weekend? He glanced at his watch. He really had to get going or he'd be late for his test. "Well, I'll turn on this TV for you. Nickelodeon, is that right? Yep - here's good old SpongeBob. Lots of colors and sounds for you dudes to enjoy. You're not going to give me any satisfaction this morning, are you? Can't convince you to step out and show yourselves?"

Nothing. Professor Holmby had joked about finding extra guinea pigs around, but what if, really, there were fewer around? Like none? Max felt a little panicked at the thought. "Please give me a sign that you're here, okay?"

Nothing but silence.

"Okay. Well, later will work, if that's how you want to play this. Think about it while I'm gone. Think of a way to show me that you're here and okay. Okay? Well, see you later little dudes. Please - uh - eat stuff, okay? Be okay. If you're in there, don't leave while I'm gone. Okay?"

The front door clicked shut and Teddy and Pip came thumping out from their hiding place, squeaking, squealing, and screaming at the top of their little voices. And, of course, heading straight for the food.

"WORST OF TIMES IS BEING QUIET!" Pip screamed. *"NO GOOD IS WAITING WHILE NO-GOOD MAX TALKS AND TALKS ABOUT HOW WE ARE NOT SMART AND HE THINKS WE ARE NO GOOD!"*

"Pip, we are doing what we need to do and must keep up the behaving this way. But for now we can get talking and noise-making out of our systems. And also eating! Hooray!"

They gobbled everything up quickly, then lay down to rest. It had been a very trying morning staying quiet and out of sight.

Pip sighed. *"WHAT WILL WE DO? WE ARE VERY MUCH STUCK WITH A NO-GOOD HUMAN FOR DAYS AND DAYS AND WEEKS AND MONTHS! MAYBE WE ARE STUCK FOREVER! MAYBE OUR WALLY AND AMELIA WILL NEVER COME BACK AND NO MORE MOLLY JANE AND WE WILL ALWAYS AND ONLY HAVE NO-GOOD MAX!"*

Teddy nodded his unhappy agreement. *"We cannot let that bad thing happen, Pip. We will need a very good plan."*

"A PLAN TO MAKE THAT MAX GO AWAY AND BRING OUR WALLY BACK FROM HIS MINI SODA!" Pip agreed. *"MAX MUST GO, WALLY MUST COME - WORST OF TIMES CHANGES TO BEST OF TIMES!"*

"A plan," Teddy said thoughtfully, giving his left ear a good scratching. *"A good, good plan...."*

"WHAT IS THE PLAN?" Pip screamed.

"Pip, be quiet! The plan is still in the back, back of my very busy head. I have not got it out just so far.

Please let me think," Teddy said, shaking his head. *"You are too crazy some of the time. Much of the time."*

"PIP WILL GO AND DO SINGING, THEN! GOODBYE!"

Teddy groaned, and started to walk slowly down the walkway toward the living room window, thinking about a plan. A very good plan that would make Max go away and bring back Wally. Behind him, he could hear Pip squeaking out a song.

No day is good with Mom Jane in it.
Mom Jane puts everyone in buckets.
No day is good with Mom Jane in it.
Mom Jane doesn't like guinea pigs.
No day is good with Mom Jane in it.
But Wally and Amelia don't believe me.
No day is good with Mom Jane in it.
But Pip is me and I saved the day!
The end.

"We will have to make the time of Max being here the thing of 'unpleasant,'" Teddy muttered to himself. *"Not so much that he does a crazy thing, like leaving without getting Wally back firstly, but unpleasant so he will call our Wally to come back soon."* A few steps later, he stopped. A pretty good plan had come into his mind. *"Tee hee!"* Teddy started walking back toward Pip.

Max is no good.
He does not do what he should.
Max must go.
This I know.

Pip is saving the day.
Teddy says o-kay.
Max must go
This I know.

"Pip be quiet and hear what I have to say. Go turn off that loud TV so we can have a meeting about my plan."

Chapter Nine
Friday Afternoon

Max decided that he had probably passed the test, at least by a little bit. And that was good enough for him. He did not plan to be an economist or whatever for a living. He was glad to get Economics over with and move on. He wasn't good at that kind of thing, that's all. Not everyone was cut out for... everything. Every person had their thing. Economics was not his thing, so it was added to the pile of other not-his-things.

He pulled his car into the little garage at Professor Holmby's house and turned off the engine. He sat for a few minutes, enjoying the fact that there was nothing he had to do. He didn't need to take care of the bird until tomorrow. All he had to do with the guinea pigs was feed them in about three hours. So that meant sweet freedom.

He would start his free time with a nap. He deserved one after being up and at 'em painfully early taking people to the airport and such. Max got out of the car and opened the door that led into the kitchen. The house was very quiet. Too quiet. Hadn't he left that TV on? Sure he had. He had turned it on for the guinea pigs to watch SpongeBob. And now it was off. How could that be?

The guinea pigs were still totally quiet and Max wondered if they were being totally quiet on purpose just to freak him out. Did guinea pigs have devious little minds like that? Probably not. No, definitely not. They were probably scared. They were scared because he was someone new to them. He would have to be real careful with the timid little creatures, that's all. Talk quietly, move slowly. Stuff like that. The poor little things.

He checked the area in front of the house and saw, to his relief, that the dishes were all empty. Empty and also turned upside down and stuff. There was also a bunch of hay scattered around on that walkway. Huh. And on the floor too, actually. All over the living room.

Max supposed that he would need to clean that up. He scratched his head. The professor had said that he probably wouldn't have to do any cleaning. He had said that the guinea pigs liked to eat their food way too much to ever, like, toss it around like that. But that's what they had done, and it was all over. The house definitely did not look like it had last night, so he had better get it back to shipshape.

"But," he said out loud, "they ate the veggies I put out for them. They didn't, like, spread that stuff around or drop it on the carpet. That means they are alive and well. And here in this house somewhere. That's a big score for my side."

As Max searched the closets on the main level for something that looked like it could suck up hay, he heard a small sound.

"*Pssst!*"

He stopped and listened, but did not hear it again. He went back to searching the closet, and heard it again.

"*Pssst!*"

"What is that?" He asked out loud. "It's... strange," he muttered, shaking his head. He stood still and listened but didn't hear it again. He looked around nervously, suddenly not liking to have his back to the rest of the room so much. Molly had said something about this place being haunted. Not that he believed in that stuff. No way. "Ah ha! Here's the machine I need!" he said, hauling a big Kirby vacuum cleaner out of the closet. "This thing looks like it could slurp up, like, just about anything."

And so Max prepared for vacuuming, which was not a thing that he was cut out for. (Not everyone *is* cut out for vacuuming, you know.) He searched the living room for an outlet and found plenty, but all were being used. He unplugged a lamp which did not seem to want to be unplugged and nearly toppled one of Amelia's fragile vases in the process. Finally accomplishing the plugging-in part, Max looked all around on the machine for a switch to flip on. When he finally hit the right button the machine roared to life. It was almost too loud after the complete silence, and Max felt worried about scaring the already scared little guinea pigs deeper into hiding. He didn't want the little dudes to have little panic attacks or anything.

He could picture himself rushing them to an emergency room, the poor little things being put on stretchers or whatever.... He wondered where a nearby hospital even was.

Max switched off the vacuum cleaner. He crept over to the house, where he assumed they were hiding, and peered in. "You little dudes okay in there?" he whispered. "This big noise is called *cleaning*, which I have to do since you, like, dropped stuff on the carpet. So, uh, just chill for a few minutes. It'll be over soon and you'll be okay. It's not going to hurt you. Don't have panic attacks, okay? 'Cuz I don't know where a hospital is. Maybe plug your little ears for a while if the sound, like, scares you, okay?"

There was, of course, no reply. Absolutely no sign of them. Nothing at all. Max shrugged. "I'm turning it back on now," he said.

In spite of his belief that it would be able to suck up anything, the Kirby seemed to reject a bunch of hay, making the whole vacuuming experience unsatisfying. Max turned off the noisy machine and studied the results. The room was definitely not back to the way it had looked the night before, so there was no choice but to pick up the rejected hay by hand.

"Hey, little dudes? How about we agree not to, uh, drop the hay over the edge anymore, okay? 'Cuz it's kind of an ordeal for me to, like, clean it up. I'm not really the type of dude who is cut out for cleaning, see. It really isn't my thing. So from now on, maybe just eat the hay, okay? Or leave it where it is if you have issues with it. Deal?"

Thoughts of eating made Max work faster. The sooner he got the room back to yesterday's perfectness, the sooner he could chow. Eating was very important to Max. Almost as important as sleeping. Maybe a tie.

After depositing handfuls of the dropped hay into the kitchen garbage, Max opened the fridge to check out the grub situation. Very nice! He piled up a gigantic celebratory sandwich of ham, cheese, lettuce, tomato, and mayonnaise, cut it in half, then opened a Coke. "Ah! Awesome couch time and well-earned TV-watching!"

"Pssst!"

Max poked his head through the doorway, his eyes searching all around the room. "What *is* that?" he muttered, making his way slowly to the couch.

"PSSST!"

Max turned his head toward the sound, but saw nothing. He shook his head. "Never mind that, Max old boy. It is time to r-e-l-a-x!" He set paper towels carefully on the coffee table and even more carefully moved a knick-knacky doodad aside. Then he turned on the TV.

The professor and his wife had a pretty small TV. He supposed that was not too strange, since he was a professor and she was a writer. A couple of book-people like them probably didn't spend much time watching TV. They probably thought it rotted a person's mind or whatever. They read books for *fun*. They read books to their guinea pigs for fun. That kind of person did not watch a lot of TV. Except for educational shows, probably. Maybe educational shows didn't need to be watched on a big screen. Those guinea pigs actually had a bigger TV set than the humans in this house. Most unusual, Max thought. But live and let live. He found Jeopardy and took a big bite of his awesome sandwich.

He enjoyed the most excellent sandwich, the fizzy Coke, and the game show. When the food was gone, his mind started to numb, his eyes to droop. And before long, he was sound asleep.

Teddy and Pip padded quietly along the walkway, stopping behind Max's sleeping form. When they stood up and peeked over the walkway ledge, they could look down at his face. He was snoring. They gave each other a look and shook their heads. *"Lazy Max is not going to sleep in peace for very long, Pip. He must not have the feeling of wanting to stay here in this house. It is time for the unpleasant to start,"* Teddy whispered.

And Pip said, *"TEE HEE!"*

"No good," Teddy said in a medium voice. Not too loud, not too soft. He waited a few seconds, then said it again. *"No... good."*

Pip whispered in his higher squeakier voice, *"NO GOOD!"*

"No squeaking!" Teddy whispered.

"NO GOOD!" Pip said again, a little less squeakily.

"No good!"
"NO GOOD!"
"No good!"
"NO GOOD!"

"*No... good!*"

"*MAX IS NO GOOD!*" Pip said his last words just a bit too loud and Max sat up.

The guinea pigs ducked down behind the ledge quickly.

Max jerked his head from side to side. "Huh? What was that? Wassup?"

It was difficult for Teddy and Pip to stay still since they were shaking with fits of guinea giggles.

"Weird," Max breathed. "Hearing things." Then he lay back down and went back to sleep.

"*Time to do more hay dropping!*" Teddy whispered. "*Max did not like the clean-up, so let us do as much as we can, Pip! Come on, hurry!*" They hauled no-good-for-eating-anyway straw in their mouths away from the pile by the house and to the back of the couch. When the pile was nice and big, they began to pick up and push hay over the ledge so it landed on the couch, the floor and the back of Max's neck.

"*TEE HEE! THIS IS SOME FUN!*"

"*Tee hee!*" Teddy agreed. "*That was a good shot, Pip!*" He pulled another piece up over the ledge, then let it go. This one landed on Max's shoulder. More and more pieces made their way up and over the ledge and landed either on the couch or somewhere on top of Max.

When Max and the area around him had enough hay, the guinea pigs moved to another part of the room. As the nap went on and on, the room returned to the way it had looked when Max had walked in after his test.

"DUDE! WE ROCK!" Pip squeaked.

"We rock indeed," Teddy agreed, sounding tired. *"It is time for us to do some resting, Pip."*

But Pip wanted to finish with a big finale. He managed to drag an apple core over to the spot behind Max. Teddy shook his head about the idea, but Pip lifted the gooey thing anyway and shoved it up and over the edge. It landed with a juicy thunk right on Max's head.

"Huh?" Max sat up, brushed at his hair, and sprang to his feet. "What? Huh? Hey - yuck! What the...?" Straw was falling off of him. Like, lots of it. It was all over the couch this time, too. "What the...?" he said again. He picked up the apple core and studied it, wrinkling his face in disgust. "Who...?" He shook his head, looked all around him, then he started walking slowly back to the guinea pig house, checking the ledge along the way. There was no sign of them as usual. Just all of that mess.

Teddy and Pip had quietly made their way into the kitchen and were in the corner by the window working very hard at stifling giggles.

"Whoa," Max said, finally giving up the search for them with a shrug. "Weirdness." He threw the disgusting apple core into the kitchen garbage, not noticing that Teddy and Pip had scurried out of the kitchen and back to their house just as he entered. "You dudes are, like, really ambitious," he said. "I mean, that has to be a lot of work, making a big mess like that. Twice in one day. Wouldn't you rather watch

TV? I'll turn it back on for you." He debated about getting out the vacuum again. Then he heard that noise. This time he thought he heard words, too.

"*Pssst!*"

"*NO GOOD!*"

"*Pssst!*"

"*NO GOOD!*"

He stood very still and listened, frowning. Max shook his head. "This day keeps getting weirder," he said, deciding to go ahead and hand-pick the hay instead of hauling out that noisy vacuum again and risking damage to the doodads. He brought the kitchen garbage with him then started the manual chore. "How about we don't drop apples anymore, okay? Your lady friend has all kinds of delicacies in this room that might, you know, break if an apple hits them. So let's not do that anymore. Okay, dudes?"

It took quite a while to pick up all the hay. And that made Max wonder just how long it had taken those guinea pigs to drop it all. He hadn't been asleep *that* long, had he? What time was it, anyway?

Chapter Ten
Friday Evening

Max put the weirdness of the afternoon aside and began to happily think about dinner. He was not the kind of dude who let weirdness get him down. He did not even let stuff like cleaning get him down. He could bounce back with the best of them, and he was bouncing now. He would get the guinea pigs' dinner taken care of first, since they didn't mind an early timeframe, and then concentrate all of his brain waves on his own. There was a lot to choose from as far as his options, including take-out of all types. And that fact made him quite happy.

Max smiled as he pulled out the veggies in the plastic baggie labeled 'Friday Dinner.' Even though the professor had made this job pretty much a no-brainer, he did need to rinse, dry and then tear the stuff into pieces for the little dudes. He tore off some paper towels and got right to it. He had worked as a salad-prep guy at this restaurant for a whole week, so Max knew a thing or two about working with veggies.

Meanwhile, back in guinea pig headquarters....

"THIS DAY OF JOKES AND TRICKS ON MAX WAS BEST OF TIMES! MUCH, MUCH FUN!" Pip squeakily whispered. *"TEE HEE HEE! I AM WANTING TO LAUGH NOW!"*

Teddy, too, was stifling laughter. *"Pip, I agree and too have the laugh-need, but we need more to be very quiet. The big surprise for that Max comes later and now it is time for eating. It is best for us not to be interfering with him when he does the dinner!"*

"YES, YOU ARE RIGHT!" Pip squeaked. *"OUR DINNER IS MOST IMPORTANT OF ALL! WE WILL NOT DO THE INTERFERING NOW! WE WILL DO IT LATER!"*

But being quiet was really hard when plastic bags rattled, the refrigerator door opened and closed, and good smells hit their noses.

"Do not come running!" Teddy whispered. *"Remember to wait and wait until he is far gone from our sight! Remember! I know it is not in our natures, but it is important, Pip!"*

Max set the food bowls by the house and waited. And again, they did not appear as the professor had assured him they would. It was almost like... well, like they were holding back on purpose. And that was a crazy thing to think. Like they were not eating, not doing something that is totally, like, instinct, just to freak him out. They were little bitty animals. They did not have devious minds like that. No way. Right?

Max gave them ten more seconds then headed back to the kitchen to see about his own dinner. He stood in front of the opened fridge for a long satisfying while. He imagined different dinner options and combinations. He could do a frozen pizza or two frozen pizzas. He could have a pizza *and* another sandwich. He could also zap one of those Hungry Man dinners in the freezer. That might be good. But also, there was the option of using that extra cash and doing some take-out. He had a hankering for orange chicken. No, beef and broccoli. Yeah. That would be awesome. Then maybe a frozen pizza later.

Max suddenly had an idea - one that had nothing to do with his dinner. He would sneak up on those guinea pigs. Heh heh. Catch them off guard when they thought he was in the kitchen. That would be how he would get his first visual of the little dudes. Leaving the fridge door standing open, he tip-toed to the doorway and peeked into the living room.

And there they were; two guinea pigs, eating. He grinned as he watched them slurp up their professionally prepared dinner. All was well.

Smiling, Max slipped back to the fridge and closed the door. He checked the amount of cash that had been left for dial-up food, found it to be plentiful, and picked up the phone.

"D. Fong's. Can I help you?"

Max opened his mouth, but instead of placing his order for beef and broccoli, he said nothing and dropped the phone. Because out of the blue, out of absolutely nowhere, the most unexpected and totally loud noises started up.

Those guinea pigs were standing on their back legs, side by side, leaning against the walkway ledge, screaming their little heads off. It was more noise than he ever imagined critters that small could make. It didn't seem... right. Or possible. But that's what was going on. One of them actually sounded like an ambulance siren. The whole thing was, like, totally shocking to the system.

Max retrieved the phone and held it back up to his ear. The order-taker from D. Fong's was saying, "Hello? Hello? Is someone there?" Then he hung up.

Max hung up too.

And those guinea pigs went immediately silent and stood staring at him, innocently.

He stared back. "Well... huh," Max said, scratching his head. "Hello to you too, fuzzy little dudes. Decided to come on out and say a big noisy howdy, huh?" He gave a little chuckle then redialed D. Fong's number.

But just as he was about to give his order, the same bizarro thing happened. The guinea pigs started screaming their heads off! It was almost like they didn't want him to get Chinese food. Like, really, really didn't want that.

"Hey, dudes, could you maybe, uh...." Max yelled over the ruckus, "... shhh?" But the order-taker had already hung up so Max put the phone down. He crouched so he was eye-to-eye with the screaming critters. "So, what's up little dudes?" he asked. "You, like, totally hide and ignore me and now suddenly you want to talk *real loud* while I'm trying to get some chow? What gives? You got something against D. Fong's?"

The guinea pigs stared silently.

"Okay. So you want some attention now? Good enough. Here you go - howdy. I'm Max. And I'm here to take care of you dudes until Monday."

Pip made a little squeak.

"I will totally hang with you, if that's what you want, in just a minute. Here's the immediate deal: I need some chow and I want Chinese food. That means I need to order it up, like, over the phone. You guys understand about chow, right? Like, it's real important. So can we talk or scream at each other a little later on? I need a minute to make a call. Okay? Just a minute, dudes."

Teddy and Pip stood silently staring as Max reached for the phone again. He began to slowly back away, out of the kitchen and into the living room. They followed, walking slowly along the walkway.

"You dudes aren't gonna, like, do that screaming again are you?" Max asked over his shoulder. "Right?" He pressed the redial button. The call about to be picked up....

Strike three.

Max ordered his dinner from the front yard, which worked out okay. It wasn't raining or anything, and there weren't too many bugs. In the end, he had his food and all was well.

Since eating at the coffee table was nerve-wracking, what with all the fragile doodads in there, Max decided to eat in the kitchen. It wasn't exactly like eating all alone in silence because the guinea pigs followed him in there and watched. They continued with their conversation; squealing or whooping randomly and loudly. The little guinea pig had a knack for letting out a piercing siren-like scream just as Max was about to take a bite, startling him into dropping the food. His shirt got, like, all messed up.

Friday night dinner was an adventure.

The noisy part of Teddy's plan was big fun for them. But Max was too slow of an eater, or too big of one, compared to themselves. They grew tired. It was a good idea to spend some time on their cushions getting some rest. Tonight there was a lot more action to come.

Pip sang softly:

Max likes food.
Max calls Pip a dude.
Max does it wrong.
This is his song.
WE HAVE HAD NO READING TODAY!

Max likes food.
Max calls Pip a dude.
Max does it wrong.
This is his song.
WE HAVE HAD NO TV TONIGHT!

After the delicious but hardly relaxing dinner, Max sat on the guest room bed, pondering the night ahead. After the recent noisy turn of events, anything could happen, like, at any time, couldn't it? They could possibly decide they needed to make that kind of racket at two a.m. for example. That would be a bad deal. Max closed the door, testing it for sound-proofing. But it was hard to tell when they weren't making any noise.

Professor Holmby had said they were always quiet at night, but he also said they for sure came running when food was put out. They hadn't done that so far. "Dude, you are getting paranoid," he said to himself. "They are *guinea pigs*. They aren't exactly plotting and scheming against you behind your back. They don't have those kinds of devious minds. No way."

Having decided that, Max left the bedroom. The night would be fine. The guinea pigs would be quiet. All would be well. Now he just had that other phone call to make.

Calling a girl was not a simple thing. It was not a normal, natural thing. If it was, he would have done it long ago, wouldn't he? It was definitely not something Max was cut out for or good at. But he had to do it anyway. Just thinking about Sophie made him feel like his tongue was too thick for his mouth. How was he supposed to talk with that going on? It was a bit of a problem, actually.

He had wanted to talk to Sophie for... how long had it been, anyway? He first noticed her at orientation, back in... September? August? Geez! Almost nine months ago?! He was way too slow in the girl department. Like, turtle-speed. *Nine months? Really?*

It was a perfect time to make the call. Here he was, in a clean - well, relatively clean - house all weekend. He could invite her over to talk without Alex being around. Alex was cut out for asking girls on dates, but he was also a total slob and, like, talked too much.

He could do this. He could make the call. He needed to think for a while. He paced around the downstairs of the little house, carrying his cell phone, flipping it open, then closing it again – open, close. He sat and tapped his fingers nervously on the phone for a little while, then paced for a longer while, practicing what he was going to say.

"Hey, Sophie! It's me, Max. You know, from... that class... that we had together... that time." Max smacked himself in the forehead. He couldn't say *that*. That was insane. What *was* the class they had had together? He needed to have more information or he'd sound like someone Sophie would not want to get together with. Ever. Algebra? Was that it? He didn't remember taking Algebra. Wasn't that a class in high school? But... was that it? It seemed like that was it. He couldn't just say he was Max, this dude who kept looking at her in the cafeteria or at all the campus events. That would make him sound like a weirdo-stalker type. Algebra. Sure, it was Algebra. That was it. "Hey, Sophie! It's me, Max, from Algebra." He bravely opened up the phone. Next, he pulled the crumpled piece of paper from his back pocket. Then he punched in the number and waited, holding his breath.

"Max is not the thing of smooth with ladies," Teddy whispered.

"HE IS BUMPY, DUDE," Pip agreed.

"The Sophie will not be happy to talk to not-smooth Max," Teddy continued. *"WE WILL SAVE THE DAY FOR THE SOPHIE!"* Pip whispered. *"COME ON!"*

The guinea pigs appeared, seemingly from out of nowhere, and did a repeat of the earlier sirens, whoops and screams. They were so loud that Max dropped the cell phone. It landed on the floor just like the Professor's phone had and Max cringed. He hoped it wasn't toast. He snatched it up quickly, but - too late. Sophie surely had heard the sirens and other loud, odd sounds.

"Ugh! A weirdo!" Max heard her say before she ended the call.

"Well... that's just great," he sighed, slumping onto the couch. "Now, thanks to your bad timing, dudes, she has the number of my cell phone in her call log, so if I call back, she'll know it's the 'weirdo' again. And what are the odds that she'll not hang up, like, immediately if I call again?"

Teddy and Pip were standing together staring at Max, shaking their heads slowly from side to side.

"Dudes, imagine if there was a really pretty girl guinea pig that you wanted to talk to. Like, were dying to talk to. Or scream at. Or whatever you do. Okay? Imagine that. That's Sophie. Except she is a person, not a guinea pig. She's got this hair... and these eyes... and this smile...." Max groaned. "She is totally cool, but also sweet. So pretty. And smart! Here's the thing, okay? I need to make a call without ruckus in the background. Talking outside is somewhat uncool because there are, like, people out there doing yard work and totally staring at me and stuff. So I'm kinda begging here. Okay? After this call, we'll hang out and... scream or whatever. Together. Okay? Just give me a few minutes. Can you do that?"

Teddy and Pip did not respond at all.

Max went into the kitchen to use that phone.

Teddy and Pip followed him.

Max wandered out of the room.

They followed.

"Dudes," Max muttered, as he dialed the number again, walking away from them faster.

This time, before ending the call, Sophie said he had better not call again or she'd find out who he was and call the police. And she meant it.

Max felt his *live and let live* calmness start to shift on him. This was uncool. This was starting to get on the old nerves, actually. "All right, you guinea pigs, now the authorities are involved. Potentially. And I'm telling you, if I am going down, I'm taking you two down with me. I'm sure they have jails made just for little critters like you," Max said to – no one. The guinea pigs were silent and nowhere to be found now.

"TEDDY! WE ARE IN BIG DANGER OF JAIL NOW! WORST OF TIMES IS DOING TIME!" Pip's voice was a squeaky whisper. *"I COULD NOT MAKE IT ON THE INSIDE!"*

"Pip, guinea pigs are not put in jails. If we were, we could get out anyway because of our small nature. There no handcuff small enough, and besides, we have much knowing of Judge Judy, so we

are fine. However, though, Max is truly dangerous as we had thought. We must save the pretty, smart Sophie from weirdo Max! She is in great danger! And then we must make dangerous Max go away so our Wally will come home!" Teddy whispered back. *"It is a situation more serious than we ever thought! But for now we need rest. There is much more to do, Pip. Much more to do."*

Max stood outside on the front step, house phone in hand. It was not completely private out there, but the chances were a lot better of getting through the call without interference. "Okay, Max, here you go," he said to himself. Then, after a deep breath, he dialed again.

Sophie's phone rang and rang. Finally, there was an invitation to leave a voicemail message. After the beep, Max stumbled one out.

"Hey, Sophie, this is Max. Grantburg. Max Grantburg. From that, uh, that Algebra class? At school? So I'm not a weirdo or a stalker. Heh heh, see, I'm.... It's a long story, and it involves really noisy, but totally, uh, cute little, um, guinea pigs... and.... Say, I'm wondering if we could, you know, get together. To talk and stuff. Just for a while, to, you know, get to know each other. Because I was always hoping to... get to know you better. Anyway, I am, like, house-sitting for these people who have guinea pigs... guinea-pig sitting... and the address is, uh... hang on." Max checked the number. "It's 526 Taylor Drive, and I'll be here until Monday. So... I mean, if you wanted, you could stop by and... hang out. You could see the, uh, guinea pigs, which are cute. We could have a snack, too. During the day when it's light. Because.... So. Um... you don't have to call first, but if you want to you can. I'll just be here, hanging out, you know. It doesn't have to be a big deal, like a date, or anything, just a stop-by thing. To get to know each other. So that's it. I hope you don't still think I'm a stalker or anything. You can ignore this whole thing, but please don't have the police come here or anything. That would be, like, totally uncool... well, you know. I'll leave you alone if that's what you'd prefer. Bye. This was Max... Grantburg. From Algebra."

Back inside, Max collapsed on the couch with a groan. "You dudes honestly should've stopped me once and for all." He sat up and looked around. "Dudes? Seriously?" While he had been outside, embarrassing himself with that phone message, the guinea pigs had totally messed up the living room again.

Max stopped picking up hay and grabbed the phone from the coffee table. He accidentally bumped a statue thingamajig in his rush to answer. It was a statue of a little girl holding an umbrella with a delicate-looking stick, or stem... or whatever it was that umbrellas had, and it teetered most dangerously. Max caught it at the last second, setting it upright with a big sigh of relief. "Sophie?" he gasped into the phone.

A kindly, definitely male chuckle confirmed that it was not. "Wally, actually. Sorry to disappoint. How is it going, Max?"

"Professor! Hey! How are you? How is Minnesota? Is it, like, snowing there?"

"It is actually quite balmy here, being May and all," he chuckled.

"Right. Of course. So... what's up?"

"Just checking in, my boy. Is everything all right?"

"You bet. Yep. Everything is all right." Max looked around the room at the hay that was... everywhere. "We spent some, like, quality time together today."

"Good, good to hear. So they decided not to continue hiding from you?"

"Yep, they came out, that's for sure. They had a lot to say - once they came out of hiding."

"A lot to *say*?" The professor sounded concerned about that.

"You know, a lot of, like, loud screaming, or whatever you call it. Not screaming, but, like, loud sounds. You know."

"Good to hear! Wonderful!"

"Yeah, it's, like, really wonderful," Max muttered.

"I don't suppose they'd be interested in having a word or two with me?"

Max frowned. "Huh? Seriously? I mean, no sweat. Sure thing, Professor, let me take a look around to see where they're at. They don't exactly come when I call or anything. And, I mean, if they see me with a phone in my hand, you just never know what might happen...." Max's voice trailed off as he walked around the room. "Uh, dudes, if you want to come on out, the professor would like to talk at ya," he said.

To his amazement, Teddy and Pip came thumping out from hiding. They leaned up against the ledge and made rather pleasant and soft whooping sounds.

Max uncovered the mouthpiece. "Well, what do you know? Here they are, Professor. Front and center and ready to be talked at."

"Good to hear!"

"I'll hold the phone up to their little heads and you can... talk away. Okay?"

Wally chuckled. "Actually, if you would be so kind as to gather our mail for us, Max, I failed to ask last night. You can simply set the phone down somewhere in the vicinity of Teddy and Pip while you walk out to the mailbox. I do thank you for indulging me. You must think Amelia and me a bit eccentric in our dealings with our boys. To say the least."

"Nah, you're cool. It's no problem, Professor. Live and let live; that's my motto."

"An admirable motto, Max."

"I'm setting the phone down now and I'll go grab the mail and be right back."

The guinea pigs approached, nosing the phone with great interest. "Behave yourselves. No screaming now. This is your old buddy the professor here, not some food place or some *girl I totally like*."

The guinea pigs ignored him.

Max headed for the door.

"Teddy? Pip? Are you there? Has Max left the house?" Wally chuckled. "It is so good to talk to you, boys! Tell me how it is going."

Teddy won the first round of pushing and so he had the first words. *"Wally!"* he began frantically. *"We need you to come home! You need to come back right now! Max is no good!"* he squealed. *"He is having a big party which is not okay! And also he is a weirdo stalker and now the Sophie is in great danger!"*

"Theodore, what in heaven's name are you talking about? I do not hear a party going on. Pip? Are you there? I need a second opinion."

"Second opinion hurts my feelings," Teddy pointed out. *"It means you are not believing me and possibly are calling me a liar."*

"I apologize if I am hurting your feelings, my boy. But I also believe you are handing me a slight fabrication and that is not okay. And you know that."

"MAX IS NO GOOD! WALLY, COME HOME! NOW!!!" Pip squealed. *"TEDDY IS NOT HANDING YOU ANY FABRIC! MAX IS HAVING A BIG BIG PARTY! HE IS DOING IT ALL WRONG! HE IS BAD LIKE BARBARA AND MOM JANE! YOU NEED TO SAVE US!"*

"According to Max, everything is just fine."

"Wally, possibly Max is the one doing fabricating. Surely you believe your best friends and not that Max who is a weirdo stalker!"

"Is he is feeding you? Giving you water and hay? Keeping you safe?"

The guinea pigs did not answer. *"Max is no good. Wally has to come home,"* Teddy repeated. *"The Sophie is in great danger!"*

"I am sure that I have no idea what you are talking about," Wally chuckled. "Have you been watching a dramatic movie on television tonight? Listening to too much Harry Potter?"

"WE HAVE HAD NO READING OR TV!" Pip shrieked.

"Is this true? Did Max fail to turn on your cartoons this morning?"

"MAX IS NOT GOOD FOR US AND HE NEEDS TO GO! NOW OR SOONER!"

"Now!" Teddy chimed in.

"Boys, let us be kind."

Silence.

"Max is Molly's cousin, and we love and trust Molly, don't we? Therefore, if she trusts and believes Max, so must we."

"OBJECTION!"

"Molly Jane does not know of Max's weirdo stalker behaving!" Teddy said. *"Molly Jane needs to know. Call her in Florida and tell her to come home, too! Everyone needs to come home!"*

"Boys, honestly," Wally interrupted. "I believe in Max and his goodness. You will have to give me a much more specific, and dare I say intelligible, explanation before I come dashing home. It appears that all is very well indeed."

"ALL IS NOT WELL INDEED!" Pip shrieked.

"Max did not read to us today, not one word!"

"Ah, well. Is that really the worst thing that could happen, Theodore?"

"It is not okay, Wally! You told that Max to read to us and he did not do it!"

"Naturally, you prefer life as usual with me, Amelia, and Miss Molly at your beck and call, but sometimes we need to make sacrifices in life. Now, I'm sure that he will be back in the house soon, so let's talk about something else in the time we have left."

"Max is having big, big parties which are not allowed, and the pretty smart Sophie is in great danger!" Teddy insisted. *"We must save the day before we all end up in jail!"*

Max whistled as he set a pile of mail on the little table next to the door. "Are you dudes still on the phone with the professor?" He grinned as he picked up the receiver, sending the guinea pigs darting in separate directions, and said, "Hey, it's me, Max. I got the mail. And your next-door neighbor dude, like, said he would mow your grass for you, if you want. Said he would be happy to and stuff. So I said maybe I should ask you about it. He wouldn't be doing that sort of thing in the early morning hours, would he?"

"Max, you can tell Mr. Peterson thank you anyway, but I will be sure to have it taken care of myself once I return." The professor sounded a bit put out about that. "I have a lawnmower of my own and am quite capable of attending to my own piece of property."

"So, like, he's *that* kind of neighbor? Dude. Too bad for you."

"Precisely. Max, my boy, do you have any questions or concerns as long as we are talking? Is everything truly going all right?"

Max hesitated. "It's fine. They just like to turn up the volume sometimes when I'm on the phone. Which was only to order Chinese and then...." He cleared his throat.

"Perhaps when you attempted a phone call to a certain young lady?"

"Perhaps," Max mumbled.

"I do apologize for that."

"No, no sweat. I'm over it. I'm sure she doesn't, like, totally think I'm a... dangerous sicko. She won't call the police or anything. Probably."

Wally's chuckle was sympathetic.

"It's okay, Professor. No sweat." Max raked at his hair.

"Is there anything else you would like to discuss?" Wally asked kindly.

"Well, uh, like, if the guinea pigs, you know, happen to throw some hay, like, over the edge of that walkway in the living room area... I mean, I'll clean it up for sure, but should I be vacuuming it up or, like, do it by hand?" Max was surprised to hear Wally laughing merrily at this question. "Professor?"

"I apologize, Max, but that is such an image! I cannot imagine such a thing happening to a degree where a vacuum cleaner would be necessary."

"Right," Max said.

"The boys would have to take great pains to haul and lug their hay over that ledge. And they do love their hay – to eat, so it is highly unlikely."

"High unlikely, huh?"

"But if they do happen to somehow fling a piece up and over the edge, I would truly appreciate your help in picking it up by hand. I fear that the vacuum cleaner would have difficulty getting it all up and it might clog up the mechanism."

Uh oh. A clogged mechanism? He sure hoped he hadn't done that. "Yeah, imagine that. Like they'd haul that stuff around and dump it on the couch or floor on purpose."

Wally chuckled some more. "Max I do sincerely appreciate your services and it was a pleasure to catch-up with the boys. Please relax and enjoy yourself as much as you can. By the way, how did your final go?"

"Oh. Aw, well...." Max scratched his head.

"Does that mean not so well?"

"Let's just say I wish I would've spent more time talking with you, Professor, before I sat myself in that exam chair this morning."

"Ah. I see. Well, life goes on, does it not?"

"Far as I know," Max said. "Guess we'll see."

Wally chuckled. "Is the young lady you hope to entertain named Sophie by any chance?"

"Yeah, how did you...?"

"Anyway, again I thank you for your services and for keeping a watch over my boys, and I will call again tomorrow."

"You're welcome, Professor. Take 'er easy, dude!"

Chapter Eleven
Friday Night

While Max finished his clean-up of the living room, it seemed like there were little snickers coming from across the room. He imagined the guinea pigs dropping hay behind his back and laughing about it. And that, of course, was crazy thinking. They were guinea pigs. They were animals who acted on instinct. They did not have devious minds.

And he was a dude who had left a barely understandable voicemail message for Sophie. She was probably playing it over and over again for her girlfriends back at school. They were all, like, laughing their heads off at him. They had probably looked him up in the "who's who" book to see what he looked like, because the name Max Grantburg didn't ring any of their bells. They were having a good laugh about him because he was funny, in a goofy type of way. The other girls were giving Sophie advice like to never talk to him ever and definitely not to go to the house. No way. Or else they were calling the police.

Max stopped his cleaning and lay flat on the floor, staring up at the ceiling. What if a bunch of freshmen girls showed up here to get a look at him? That could happen. He had totally given Sophie the address. What if they were peeking in the window right now seeing him crawling around picking up stuff or lying on the floor as he currently was?

He sat up, smoothed his hair and looked carefully up at the windows. The curtains were all shut. Whew. It would not be possible to peek in. That thought put Max's mind at ease a bit. At least if they were laughing at and about him, it was from the girl's dormitory, and not at close range.

Well so much for getting to know Sophie. At least school was almost out for the quarter. She'd surely forget all about him, about all of this, over the summer. And then next year he would find someone else to be afraid to call for nine months.

Well, that was a very depressing thought.

The guinea pigs, to his surprise, had wandered out of hiding and were once again standing side by side, up on their back legs, leaning against the ledge, looking at him. Quietly this time. Almost sympathetically. Like they cared, or were sorry, which was nice. The bigger one let out a soft whoop or two. The little one tilted his head in an actually cute sort of a way.

"You guys want to be friends now?" Max asked, walking very slowly toward them. "I don't have a phone in my hand, see? Just a trash can from picking up another of your *big messes*. I didn't rat you out to the professor about that stuff. I hope you appreciate that."

The guinea pigs remained silent and still.

Max crouched down to look at them. The one called Teddy whooped softly, and Max reached out a tentative hand and was surprised to be allowed to pet his head.

The other one pushed Teddy aside and got his little head under Max's hand.

Max grinned. "Oh, I think I get it. This day was like Freshman Orientation or something. Initiation, I mean. Now we're done with the pranks and I'm in the club? Is that right?"

Teddy was now the one being petted. Max shook his head. "Okay, I'll admit you're cute - when you're like this, for example. How about let's call a truce? Can we do that? Do you know what a truce is? Let's have one. Especially during the overnight sleeping hours. Okay? You dudes understand and respect sleep, right?"

The guinea pigs allowed him to pet them for a while longer, making quiet noises. Then they waddled off toward their house, leaving Max smiling after them.

He flicked off the lamps, then headed for the frilly blue bedroom. It had been a long, exhausting day, and he was so ready to snooze.

"Pip, Max is not done with this day like he thinks," Teddy said quietly.

"WHY WERE WE BEING THE THING OF NICE TO THAT MAX JUST NOW?! THAT SEEMS LIKE NOT A GOOD OR RIGHT PLAN!"

"We have done the thing called 'lulling into a false sense of security' with that last trick. He will not expect what is coming next."

"OH! TEE HEE! LULLING IS MUCH FUN! LULLING IS LIKE TRICKY TRICKING!"

"Pip, shhh!"

"SHHH!" Pip repeated with a giggle.

"Remember - you are to only say "booooooo"! That is all you get to say for now. Nothing else! No crazy Pip-talk or singing at this time because it will give us away too much. Try not to be squeaky."

"SOMETIMES WORDS OR SONGS COME OUT OF THIS MOUTH AND I DO NOT EVEN WANT THEM TO," Pip whispered. *"I WILL DO MY BEST, BUT CANNOT BE SURE."*

"Try hardest," Teddy said. *"Now, let us rest a while before we start the nextest plan. I am not sure of which number of plan we are doing now. So many plans for one day. Max is much hard work for us."*

"NOT WORK, BEST FUN TIMES!" Pip insisted. *"LULLING, SPILLING HAY, AND PHONE-SCREAMING IS MUCH, MUCH FUN!"*

Teddy asked him to *"shhh"* again, then the pair settled in for a little nap.

"Boooooo!"

"Goooooo awaaaaaay! We don't like youuuuuu!"

Max sat straight up in bed, listening hard. He shook his head to clear it, wiggled a finger in each ear, then listened more. There was nothing for a little while and then, *"Boooooo!"* and *"We don't like youuuuuu!"*

"All right, what is going on?" Max said out loud, trying to sound like he wasn't the least bit afraid or worried. Like there was no way in the world he would even think for a second that what he was hearing was... a ghost. He stepped out of the bedroom, ducked under the walkway and went into living room where he switched on a light. He stood still and listened. The noises had stopped. There was nothing. Nothing at all.

What was going *on* here? No wonder these guys paid $100 to feed guinea pigs! What a crazy gig this was! He walked over to where the guinea pigs were lying down and looked at them. They stared back at him with wide-open black eyes. Innocent eyes. He was responsible for the helpless little things and their safety. He needed to protect them from the... ghost. Or whatever it was.

It wasn't a ghost. No way.

"It's okay, little dudes. Everything is okay. Sorry I woke you up. Go back to sleep."

Teddy sniffed at him, raising his nose as if curious. Then he snuggled down and looked like he was going to go back to sleep. Pip was up on all four legs, very alert, but very quiet. Max shook his head, then switched off the light and stood very still again.

He did *not* believe in ghosts or anything like that. He just didn't. That was crazy. He was a lot of things, but crazy was not one of them. There was an explanation. It was probably old pipes, plumbing, air flow... something. Or something, somewhere in the house was moving... things... around... somewhere. Max sat on the couch and put his head in his hands. Maybe he had an imagination after all. That would just plain figure. Of all the times in his life for that to pop up....

Maybe he would stay on the couch for a while, with the light back on....

"... *We don't like you... we don't like you... we don't like you... we don't like you... we don't like you... go a-way... go a-way... go a-way... go a-way....*"

The voices were in his dream. He was dreaming. Of course! He was dreaming all of it, probably. He was dreaming the kind of dream where you know you're dreaming. He was having one of those, and that was fine. As long as it was a dream.

There were guinea pigs in the dream. Not just the two, but loads of them creeping up on him from all over the house! He was lying on the living room floor and they were crawling on him, getting right in his face and saying, *"We don't like you. Go away!"* Some were crawling up his arms, some standing on his chest; some pushing at him with their noses, as if they could move him if they tried hard enough. There was one who seemed to be the chief guinea pig, front and center, wearing a policeman's hat, looking him straight in the eyes. And he said, *"You are a weirdo stalker and must leave the pretty, smart Sophie alone or the police will come and lock you into a jail!"* The room was absolutely full of guinea pigs now. There was no floor to walk on, even if he could stand up and run. And then Professor Holmby was there, as a voice or a ghost, saying, "Our three hundred guinea pigs are so precious to us. All of them. We love them all dearly. Please be careful with them. If any of them are harmed, we will have to call the police, Max. You understand, don't you?"

"Max is no good! Max is no good! Save Sophie! Save Sophie!" The chanting went on and on until Max woke and sat up straight. He shook himself all over and raked at his hair. He gradually realized that he was not covered in disapproving guinea pigs, and neither was the floor. He was on the couch. The two actual guinea pigs were quietly watching him over their ledge with great interest. It was silent in the house. There was no chanting. Max put his head in his hands and groaned. It was 4:30 in the morning.

Max shuffled to the bedroom, ducked, and entered. He closed the door, fell onto the bed, then put a pillow over his head. This time, he slept. Like a log. And there were no dreams to disturb him.

Chapter Twelve
Saturday Morning

Teddy and Pip had not been served their expected early-morning breakfast and were ordering it up at top volume. They were right in front of the closed door of Max's frilly bedroom, which was not as soundproofed as he had hoped.

Max sat up, disoriented, and flung back the covers, ready for action. It took several moments for his heart to slow and his head to clear. Guinea pigs wanted to be fed. That was what all the ruckus was about. There was no big emergency. All he had to do was feed them and then they would be quiet. And he could go back to sleep.

Max opened the door, ducked under the walkway, then slogged his way to the kitchen. He was followed by the guinea pigs, still doing their really loud breakfast-ordering.

"Dudes, I'm on it, okay? You can pipe down about it." Max rinsed the vegetables and soaked up the water half-heartedly and unprofessionally. He tossed the pile of soggy veggies right in front of them on the walkway so they would stop screaming. The screaming, so early in the morning, was making his head hurt.

The guinea pigs began chewing and slurping as if he had not fed them a scrap since he had arrived. Which was hardly true or fair. The wetter-than-usual greens left the white parts of their furry chins looking green. Max hoped that the greenness would wear off before the professor and his wife noticed. Would he have to try to wash their chins? That seemed like an impossible thing to have to do. The guinea pigs would never allow that. They would run away and hide for sure, so never mind.

He poured some pellets into the bowls by the house, then moved the bowls away from the edge. He did not want that green stuff to end up on the carpet. That would be a big mess. Then he filled the hay. Next, he checked the water and found it to be completely empty. Under the bottle was a very soggy pile of gray stuff.

If he were more of a paranoid type of dude, he would say they had drained all the water out on purpose, leaving a big mess for him to clean up. But that, like the other stuff, would require devious planning minds, and these were guinea pigs. Guinea pigs did not have devious planning minds. They were messy. And noisy. But not devious.

Max yawned, then got some paper towels from the kitchen. He sopped up some of the yucky gray puddle, then filled the water bottle back up. Was he missing anything? Nope, he didn't think so. He had given the guinea pigs food and water, and all was well.

Except that there was hay all over the living room again.

Never mind that. It was time for Max to go back to bed.

Of course, the neighbor dude had decided that now was the time to mow the lawn. Max hadn't told him not to, so he assumed he should. *Vrrrrooooom!* Max lay awake for twenty more minutes, then gave up on sleep.

The Saturdays of Max Grantburg never started at eight-thirty. They also did not include rude awakenings twice in one night. He would have to take a nap later to make up for the poor-quality sleep. But since sleep was impossible right now, he might as well eat.

Not usually awake early enough to fit breakfast into the day, Max wasn't sure what to eat. He stood in front of the refrigerator for a long time, feeling dazed. He enjoyed the cool air as he looked at food.

There was a little squeak, and he turned his head to see a guinea pig staring at him. "Hey," he managed, returning to his food-staring. "What do you want? I already fed you. Shouldn't you be making a mess for me to clean up or something?"

The green-chinned guinea pig squeaked again. It was only a little sound, nothing ear-splitting. Max grabbed a package of lunch meat, some cheese and mayonnaise, then closed the door. He found some bread and started assembling a breakfast sandwich.

The guinea pig squeaked a little louder this time, then started a steady *wheek wheek wheek*-ing, ending each beat in a little snort. He continued to do that suspenseful thing until Max gave the little guy his full attention. Sandwich in his mouth, he stepped up to the ramp and gave the dude a looking-over. "What's up, little guy?" he asked with a mouth full of food. "You feeling all right? Not sick or anything from the... wet salad?" Max felt a flicker of guilty concern about that. "Want me to, like, wash up your chin or something?"

The guinea pig looked left, then right, then wheeked louder.

Max looked left, then right, also. "What, little dude? What's up?"

The wheeking continued as the guinea pig stood up against the wall and increased the volume.

"Where's your companion at? Don't you guys usually stick together like glue or something?" Max asked, as another rather bad feeling washed over him. They *did* stick together like glue. They were two peas super-glued in a pod together. He had actually never seen one without the other. He was seeing only one right now, and that one was acting like... like something was up. Max chewed on the sandwich and stared at the guinea pig. "Well? Where's your buddy? Come on, this is not a good game. Go find him."

The lone guinea pig stayed still but continued the steady wheeking and snorting sounds and Max walked into the living room to do a quick look-around. There was no sign of the smaller guinea pig. What was the name? Pep? Pup? No, Pip. "Pip! Where are you, buddy?" Max called. "Come on out, dude!" He inspected the ledge and walkways, then peered into the house. He even felt around a little with his free hand. "Pip? Buddy? You in there? This isn't funny. Come on out!"

The other guinea pig began to pace frantically back and forth along the walkway. He increased that steady wheeking to a higher volume, adding to the suspense.

"Pip? Come on out, buddy, dude, fuzzy guy - where are you?"

Nothing.

"Oh... man." Max sat on the couch, very still. The non-missing guinea pig was quiet now, too, standing up on his hind legs against the ledge staring at him expectantly. He was responsible. One of the two guinea pigs was missing, and he was totally responsible. A terrible scenario was forming in Max's tired mind. What if the one called Pip had somehow gone over the ledge and fallen to the ground? What if he was hurt?

But there was no sign of him anywhere. Max had already checked.

But what if he had wandered off, limping on a hurt foot, or paw, or whatever?

The professor had left the name and number of the vet. Should he call now? Did vets make house calls? No. He needed to find Pip first so he knew what he was dealing with.

Max was feeling panic now as his eyes scanned the room for a possible hiding place. There seemed to be nothing, nowhere to hide. Well, he would just have to start looking everywhere, wouldn't he? He tossed the remainder of his sandwich onto the kitchen table, then crawled around on hands and knees, slowly, carefully, checking every possible place an injured guinea pig could be hiding out. He checked the guest room and bathroom. He checked the kitchen cabinets, even the ones he had never opened. Then he went back to the living room and started checking under the furniture, softly calling, "Pip? Pip, buddy? Make a sound if you can so I can find you, okay?"

And so Max was on the floor, on his hands and knees, hay in his uncombed hair, when the doorbell chimed. Directly above him, side by side, peeking over the edge of the walkway ledge, were... both of them. "Huh?"

They watched with great interest as Max stared. "Where in the world have *you* been?!" he managed, as he stood and made his way to the door.

He flung it open, expecting to see the lawn-mowing neighbor with a bill in his hand for his unwanted services. But to his shock and disbelief, there stood Sophie.

She flashed an uncertain smile and took a step back.

"Uh...." Max's head was spinning, his stomach swirling all over the place. "Um.... Uh...."

"Max?"

"Yes. I'm Max."

"Hello. I got your phone message." Sophie took another step back. "This is a bad time." She shook her head and turned to go. "We can... do this some other time."

"No! No, it isn't a bad time at all! Please don't... I mean, please *do*... come in. Thanks for coming. Sorry about the...." Max brushed hay off of his shoulder. "I was just... taking care of... things." They stood awkwardly for a moment. "Come in. If you want. It's a little messy right now. Sorry. I was just about to... take care of.... Come in."

"I guess I can come in for a *little* bit," Sophie said, a bit uncertainly. She stepped into the house and looked around curiously. "So, you said you're watching some guinea pigs, right?"

"Uh huh." Max moved his tongue around in his mouth experimentally. Then repeated, "Uh huh."

"I love guinea pigs. I have one of my own, you know," Sophie said, craning her neck, trying to find the guinea pigs. "Her name is Coco. She is so sweet."

"Coco," Max repeated. "Sweet."

"I do remember you, by the way, from class. It was Trigonometry."

Max grimaced at the correction. He wanted to smack his forehead, but resisted with effort. *Trigonometry! Oh yeah, that eight-o'clock class that nearly killed him....*

"I always thought you seemed... nice," Sophie said.

Max smiled and kept his mouth shut.

"Max is not nice! He is worst of times! We must save pretty Sophie," Teddy whispered, and Pip nodded vigorously. They crept out of their sleeping area and toward the living room door.

"I'd love to see them, or hold them," Sophie was saying, her mind leaving Max and his niceness and going back to the guinea pigs. "Oh my goodness, look at this room! Do they walk around in this thing? That is the coolest thing I've ever seen!" She examined the walkway. "Oh, there they are! Max, they are so cute! Look at them!"

Teddy and Pip had made their entrance and were clambering to be close to Sophie's outstretched hand. Smiling, she let them sniff her. Then they stood still and let her pet them, pushing as they jockeyed for position. Sophie giggled. "They're adorable, Max! Hi, cuties!"

"Yeah," Max managed, smoothing at his hair when she wasn't looking. "Adorable. And they seem to *like*... you."

"Can I pick one of them up?" Sophie asked, her eyes shining.

Max wanted to tell her that she could do whatever she wanted. She could take both of them home with her, actually. Whatever she wanted. Just keep on smiling like that. "I don't mind, but it's mostly up to them," he said. "They're pretty much the bosses around here. I'm just the waiter and, like, clean-up crew. Their names are Teddy and Pip, by the way."

Max braced himself as Sophie reached out to pick up the nearest guinea pig, Teddy, who had pushed Pip unceremoniously aside. To his shock, there was no problem. Sophie scooped the dude right up and he didn't scream or anything.

"Oh, aren't you a *love*!" Sophie crooned. "So soft and sweet." She cuddled Teddy close to her cheek and spoke softly. "You have a green chin. How did that happen?"

Max cringed a bit, but Teddy made a purring sound and nestled himself in Sophie's arms. Would Sophie expect him to have a similar ability with the animals? Would she expect him to pick up the other one and be all cuddly with him? Would she be impressed if he did? That would score big points, probably. He reached for Pip, who, of course, went streaking away.

Fortunately, Sophie seemed to be enjoying her cuddle with Teddy too much to notice or even remember that Max was there. For the moment, anyway, that was a plus.

Pip, growing tired of being left out, soon wandered back and began his siren sounds, which startled, but amused Sophie a great deal. "Oh *my!*" she laughed, handing Teddy to Max (who panicked as Teddy started to growl, then set the guinea pig down on the walkway). "It looks like your friend is jealous!" She stepped up to Pip, who was now screaming at top volume, and picked him up – just like that. Pip did not streak away and he stopped screaming immediately. Sophie gave him a cuddle and some petting.

Teddy began to do his steady wheeking and Max knew what was coming. Those two dudes would tag-team with Sophie. She would grab one and the other would scream, and it would go on and on. And then she would have to leave.

It went about four rounds before Sophie got firm with them. "Okay, you cuties, that is enough. I am going to see if Max has a treat for you, and then we are going to have some human time together. You can listen, but no more screaming or we will go outside."

Max grinned and gave her a thumbs up.

"Do you have any fruit for them? Like, an apple?" Sophie asked.

Remembering the goopy apple core that had landed on his head the day before Max said, "Probably," and went to the kitchen. As he rummaged in the fridge, he became horrifically aware of the fact that he was in his *pajamas*. They weren't obvious pajamas; just some gray sweatpants and a really old and faded T-shirt that said *Vote for Pedro* on it. Overall, not real classy. Plus he had not washed up or combed his hair. Would a quick change-up would be okay, essential, or rude at this point?

He decided it would be rude and possibly a waste of precious time. He grabbed an apple and a peach (or maybe it was a nectarine or something of that sort). Not sure what to do with them, he rinsed both off, dried them on his shirt, then set both fruit pieces down. The guinea pigs, at least temporarily, lost all interest in Sophie.

Sophie smiled triumphantly at Max. "Now, then, shall we have a seat?"

Max offered her food and drink, but she politely refused. She did not want to eat, she wanted to sit and chat. Which would have been awesome, but unfortunately, he was tired. He had not had the nap yet, and the fact that he looked like a total mess was not forgotten. With no distractions like TV or food, Sophie, the opposite of a total mess, was looking right at him.

"How are your finals going?" she asked brightly, her green eyes sparkling at him hypnotically.

Max stifled a yawn. "Great," he said, hoping his nose wasn't growing like Pinocchio's. "I had Econ yesterday. I did... okay. You?"

"It's hard to say. I don't think I failed anything, but, you know, didn't do my best either. Don't you hate that feeling?"

Smart people always said things like that, Max knew, even if they were really just wondering whether they got an A or an A minus. He changed the subject. "What are you doing for the summer?"

"I'll be working as a camp counselor. How about you?"

"Not sure yet," Max said. "I usually pick up some part time jobs here and there. Last summer I did some house painting." He shrugged. "Pet sitting," he added. "Stuff like that. Mowing lawns."

"That sounds... fun," Sophie said uncertainly.

"Yeah, it's okay. Hot sometimes. You know, hot weather. Painting in hot weather is... hot. And when it rains, I, like, can't work." Max started to feel really nervous about how this was going. He did not sound interesting, or smart. And he was a tired mess, too.

It was actually a good time for what happened next to happen. All of a sudden, an apple core dropped over the ledge, hit Max on the head and landed on the coffee table. It bumped the fragile umbrella-girl doodad, which began to tip. Max lunged for the doodad and caught it. Then he let out a long, slow breath of relief and said, "Whoa."

Sophie started to giggle, then it turned into laughing. She rushed to put her hands over her mouth so she would stop, but couldn't. "Oh my goodness! That was amazing!"

Max grinned and shrugged.

Overhead, Teddy and Pip were peeking at them over the ledge. Teddy dropped a mouthful of hay, which landed on the back of the couch.

Sophie could not stop herself from laughing. "Oh my gosh, that is so *cute*! Do they do this kind of thing a lot?"

"Uh... yeah," Max nodded. He could think of other descriptions for that kind of thing besides cute. But at the moment, the messy behavior was helping to cut through the tension between him and Sophie. He set the statue of the girl with the umbrella on top of the TV then returned to the couch.

The guinea pigs began to do in plain view what they had been doing in secret other times. Back and forth to the hay pile they went, dumping mouthfuls over the edge and making Sophie sparkle with laughter and delight.

Her sparkly laughter was contagious and Max started to join her. Even though what they were laughing about meant a whole bunch more cleaning for him later.

"They really love you," Sophie choked, trying to get control of herself. "They want attention, right? That's why they're doing that? Because they love you?"

"I've been on my knees cleaning this place, like, constantly. If that isn't love, I don't know what is," Max laughed.

Sophie broke up into even more laughter. "Oh! Sorry, Max - I'm so sorry! This is all just so adorable!" She wiped at her eyes. "I can't imagine Coco *ever* doing something like this!"

"Yeah, well, Coco probably likes you."

"I think they secretly love you," Sophie whispered.

"When I tried to call you yesterday, they were following me around and making lots of noise every time I tried to talk," Max shared.

She found that amusing too. "I thought it was some creepy phone stalker," Sophie said. "I'm sorry about my reaction - you just never know about that kind of thing."

"Who would ever, you know, believe it, or think of it being a guinea pig thing?" Max shrugged.

"Not me."

"Not me either, until, like, yesterday. Now I believe it."

The perimeter of the room was now fairly well coated with hay and Teddy and Pip had disappeared. Sophie wanted to inspect the rest of the guinea pigs' living quarters. She noticed every detail and loved it all. She even peeked into the guest bedroom and giggled about the frilly curtains and unmade bed.

They went into the kitchen and Max offered her something to eat. This time she agreed to a sandwich since it was nearly lunchtime. He shoved the half-eaten breakfast-sandwich into the garbage quickly, then began to set out ingredients.

"The plan is not working on pretty Sophie! That girl thinks our doings are much fun and funny and that we are doing our jokes and tricks because we have love for that Max! She is not thinking that Max is the no-good person who is making problems happen," Teddy said with a shake of his head. *"I will need to think hard on how to get her away from that dangerous Max. My little head is emptying of good plans, Pip!"*

Pip squeaked, *"I LIKE SOPHIE! SHE SMELLS OF GRASS!"*

"Shhhh, Pip, be quiet. I am doing planning now and need peace. Go do some spying on those people, please. Make trouble if you can!"

"Copy," Pip whispered, then wandered off to the kitchen. He made big siren sounds whenever Max was talking. This made the Sophie laugh and seem very happy.

But nothing he did made Sophie want to get away from Max. How could he make her see that Max was a no-good, dangerous weirdo? Pip started chewing on the top of the walkway, something Wally and Amelia asked him not to do. The chewing made a satisfyingly big sound that stopped the talking going on at the table.

"Uh oh! What's he doing now?" Sophie left her place at the kitchen table, walking away from Max's no-good, boring story about himself. "Hi, cutie!"

Pip did his biggest, loudest siren sound yet, making Sophie back up a bit, but then brought her back with a couple of soft wheeks. She giggled and cooed over him as Teddy joined them.

Max watched as the guinea pigs tag-teamed Sophie again with so-called "cute" behaviors. Sophie chattered with them and laughed and cooed, and Max, exhausted and ignored, slumped in his chair and finished his sandwich.

"How long are you going to be watching them?" Sophie asked him.

Max blinked, quickly swallowed his mouthful and asked, "Huh?"

"How long are you going to be watching Teddy and Pip?" Sophie repeated.

"Oh. Until Monday night."

"Oh, how *lucky*," Sophie sighed. "I think it would be so much fun. If you like guinea pigs, that is." She smiled.

"Yes," Max said firmly. "I like them."

Sophie turned back to the guinea pigs. "Of course you do! Who wouldn't love them?" Her cell phone began to jangle and she reluctantly set Teddy down to answer it. When the call finished, she said, "Sorry, everyone, but I have to go now. I have a study session for Western Civ at the library."

Max, too, had to study for that class. Hadn't exactly gotten started on it. He had barely opened the book all semester, to be honest. "Me too," he mumbled. "Western Civ test is on Monday. I need to study."

"I could come by tomorrow afternoon, if that would be all right with you. Would that be all right? Maybe we could study together?" Sophie offered.

Max hesitated. The last thing he wanted was for her to find out just how not-smart he was about things like Western Civ, which he knew nothing about. But he said, "Yeah, awesome!" anyway.

"Should we have lunch?" Sophie asked as they walked toward her car.

Lunch, studying, and cooing over guinea pigs could last for... hours. Max felt himself perspiring and his heart tripping a bit. "Yeah," he croaked. "Great!"

"Great," Sophie said with a smile, her green eyes sparkling. "I'll be here tomorrow, then. Around noon?"

"Noon. Great!" Max stood in the driveway for a long time after Sophie had driven away. He was in a state of shock of all kinds. He had a date with the girl of his dreams. Tomorrow. To study Western Civ.

He needed to get studying!

No, on second thought, he couldn't study. He was beyond tired. He was exhausted. There was no way he could study anything in his current state. He needed a nap. Max went back into the house, closing the door and locking it behind him.

"*Wheek! Wheek! Wheek! Wheek! Wheek! Wheek!*"

"*EEEEEOOOOOEEEEEOOOOO!*"

"*Wheek! Wheek! Wheek! Wheek! Wheek! Wheek!*"

"*EEEEEOOOOOEEEEEOOOOO!*"

The guinea pigs were at it again. The noisy greetings made him clap hands over his ears and shake his head. "Oh no, uh uh. No way, dudes!" he called. "Shh! I'm going to bed!"

The guinea pigs and their screaming followed him.

Max went into the guest bedroom and closed the door. But the sound of unhappy guinea pigs was only slightly muted. They were right outside the door and had turned up the volume.

Uncool. He so totally needed to sleep. He wondered if he could go upstairs and use the professor's bedroom. But maybe he shouldn't. There was that hinge-thingy in front of the frilly bedroom to block guinea pigs from being right outside the door. If he flipped that hinge up, at least they couldn't be exactly right in front of....

But the professor had asked him not to use it. Another dead-end. How was he supposed to get any rest? Should he go back to the dorm? No. He was supposed to stay in the house.

What to do.... He was so tired. So, so, so tired. He needed to study, and in order to study, he needed a nap. Sophie was coming back tomorrow, and he had to be smart by then. It had become a desperate situation. And desperate times called for....

Max opened the bedroom door again and was instantly face-to-face with screaming animals. He ducked under the walkway and headed for the guinea pigs' house. The house was a nice distance from the door of his sleeping quarters. If they would just go in the house and stay in there, he wouldn't be able to hear them so much. He looked back at the bedroom. The guinea pigs had followed and continued their screams.

"*Wheek! Wheek! Wheek! Wheek! Wheek! Wheek!*"

"*EEEEEOOOOOEEEEEOOOOO!*"

"Wheek! Wheek! Wheek! Wheek! Wheek! Wheek!"

"EEEEEOOOOOEEEEEOOOOO!"

Max stared down at the walkway until his eyes blurred. The walkway. That walkway - which allowed them to terrorize the entire downstairs of the house. That wonderful, terrible walkway.... If he could just....

Max tapped a finger against his teeth as an idea and a smile grew. "I know how to fix this," he said quietly. He went to the bedroom and retrieved his textbooks. He plopped Economics to the left, blocking the path to the guest room. "Ah ha!" he said, sounding crazed. His heavy copy of Western Civilization was plunked down to block the other side. "Problem solved. Enjoy some time in your humongous playhouse. You still have plenty of room to move around. Don't give me those dirty looks. Now, if you dudes will excuse me, I have an important meeting with Dr. Nap to get to. See ya later."

Chapter Thirteen
Saturday Afternoon

Naps were awesome. Max took a long one. When he woke, he stared up at the ceiling for a while. It was very quiet in the house of the professor. A house which included two incredibly noisy guinea pigs. In this situation, quiet could - and probably did - mean something really bad.

There was only one way to find out, and that involved getting out of bed.

Max closed his eyes again. Whatever was going on out there would still be going on when he finished resting. He thought about Sophie and smiled until his cell phone started ringing. The caller was Jane Fisher. He flipped open the phone. "Hey Aunt Jane! How's Mickey?"

"We are all fine, Max. How is it going for *you*? Molly demanded that we check in with you and I'll put her on in a minute. How is it going, really?"

"I... had no idea those critters were so much work."

Jane laughed and said, "I know!"

"You know?"

"Oh yes."

"It's almost like... they hate me. Personally. Is that crazy?"

"Believe me, I know the feeling."

"You do?"

"Just trust me, Max. If they seem to have it in for you, it's not your imagination. They do. And there is really nothing you can do about it except hang in there. Okay, kiddo?"

"Well, okay. I'm doing that already – hanging in there."

"Keep doing it. You'll survive. Here's Molly."

"Are Teddy and Pip okay?" Molly began.

"Hello to you, too, Mol. Oh, and thanks for asking. I am doing pretty good, considering."

"What are you talking about? Considering what? Are they okay?"

"*They* are fine, I guess. Who knows? You'd think I was torturing them constantly."

"What are they doing? Why do you say that?" Molly sounded nervous.

"Do you really want to know? There's a whole lot that they're doing. Don't you have Dumbo rides to go on and stuff?"

"We're in line for the teacups. It will be exactly four minutes and fifteen seconds before we get on - based on number of people in line and how long it takes to load up and how long the ride lasts...."

"Okay, okay, stop it smarty-pants." Max rubbed his forehead.

"I have time. So tell me what's going on."

"Well, first they tried hiding from me so I wasn't even sure they were, like, here. They only came out when I wasn't around, and just to eat, and they were totally *quiet*. Which was fine. I think I'd like to go back to those good old days. Next they started to drop hay over the edge of that skyway of theirs, like, all over the place. The professor says to me, 'As long as the place looks just like it did when we left it, it'll be cool.' It didn't look like it did when they left it at all. So I had to vacuum and pick up hay by hand. More than once. I do not excel at cleaning."

Molly giggled.

"Yeah, real funny. Then they thought it would be great fun to start piping up whenever I tried to use the phone - and I'm talking about top volume. Like, screaming at the top of their voices."

This made Molly laugh harder. "Really, Max?!"

"Yeah, really! Where's the sympathy? I'm definitely not feeling the love, Mol. It's been, like, non-stop."

"Sorry! I can imagine it all and it's very.... It's funny. Sorry."

"And then...." Max groaned. "I don't want to talk about it anymore."

"What? What happened next?"

"I think that's enough information for you. Now tell me what to do so they stop torturing me."

"I don't think there's anything you can do. Teddy and Pip make up their minds about who they like or not and don't really change them back. Just be sure that you are doing everything that Wally said. Are you reading to them?"

"You're kidding, right? *Read* to them? I don't even read to myself. They would just, like, scream their heads off while I was doing that anyway."

"They get really upset if their routine is messed up. Whatever book they're used to listening to, you should read it to them. Read them *Harry Potter*. They love it."

"Sure, no problem. I'll just read a book to a couple of guinea pigs right over their ear-splitting screams."

"Are you feeding them?"

"Mol, of course I am! Every meal, every food item. I haven't missed a thing!"

"Okay, well, I have to get in a teacup in one minute and thirty-five seconds. Here's my advice: do everything Wally said to do. Turn on their TV for them. Don't say anything that might make them mad. Pretend they're people and talk nice to them."

Max said nothing.

"Max?!"

"Okay, good advice. Go spin around. Thanks for the call."

"Bye! Tell Teddy and Pip I love them!"

"Yeah... right."

Max opened the bedroom door as quietly as he could, ducked under the ramp, then crept to the guinea pigs' house. There was no sign of them. All was quiet. Read to them? Seriously? Good grief. "Do you dudes want me to, like, read you a story?" Max asked, craning his neck around to locate them. "Dudes?" He sniffed. He wrinkled his nose. "Oh... man," Max groaned. "No way!"

The two textbooks he had so genius-ly placed in the way of their ramps were toast. He picked up the Econ book first. It was damp and missing a front cover. The pages were chewed up. There was no way he could turn it in for any used-book money at the campus book store like this. The Western Civ book was even more toast. The front cover was ripped in half, most of the pages were damp, and it was chewed up enough to be missing probably one-fourth of the information that he was supposed to know for Monday's test. Not good.

The guinea pigs wandered out to stare at him, their black eyes innocent as could be.

"Thanks. I think you have made your point, little dudes. Can we call it even now? I blocked your path and you got me back. Touché."

"WHEEK! WHEEK! WHEEK! WHEEK! WHEEK! WHEEK!"

"EEEEEOOOOOEEEEEOOOOO!"

"WHEEK! WHEEK! WHEEK! WHEEK! WHEEK! WHEEK!"

"EEEEEOOOOOEEEEEOOOOO!"

The unexpected noise made Max stumble backwards. He dropped the ruined books to the floor, then covered his ears as soon as he caught his balance.

The kitchen phone was ringing, or at least he thought it was. It was hard to make out anything above the shriekish noises coming from those destructive fuzz-buckets. Max grabbed at the phone, just in case it was ringing. "Hey, yo!"

"Max? Is that you?"

"Oh, uh, yeah! Hello, Professor!" he shouted.

"Hello, my boy! Is everything quite all right?"

Max briefly considered moving the conversation outdoors, but a peek out the window told him that the nosy neighbor-dude was plodding along with his noisy lawnmower, either still or again, right on the property line.

"I hear quite a symphony of cavy unrest!" Wally was saying. "*Is* everything all right, Max?"

"Uh...." Max made his way quickly to the guest bedroom where he could close the door, covering the mouthpiece as he went. "Things are great!" he said when he was away from the screaming. "Couldn't be better!"

"I see. Good." But it sounded like he did not believe Max at all. "Good to hear. Would you indulge me once again by setting the phone near the boys? I would like to have a word with them about their... manners."

"Huh? Oh. Okay. No problem."

"You could possibly go out and grab the mail if you haven't already done so. Perhaps a brief break from the, uh, self-expressions going on would be pleasant?" Wally chuckled.

"Okay, Professor, I'll take you up on that," Max said, leaving the bedroom and approaching the quieting guinea pigs. "I need to go feed Molly's bird anyway. So I'll be back in, like, five or ten. So talk away... to the dudes. Here you go. I'm setting down the phone now and walking away."

Max sat on the front step. His head was ringing like a bell, so the neighbor's lawn-mowing was as peaceful as church to him. He would take his time feeding the bird and getting back. This gig was starting to give him a headache.

"Boys?" Wally called. "Boys, are you there? Has Max left the room? If so, go ahead and speak!"

"Wally Wally Wally Wally Wally!"

"MAX IS NO GOOD! HE IS FIRED! HE HAS DONE TERRIBLE THINGS!"

"Max takes away our freedom and exercise and says no good things to us, Wally! We fire him! You need to come home now or sooner! The end. Thank you!"

"WE FIRE HIM! WE FIRE HIM! WE FIRE HIM! WE FIRE HIM!"

"What happened, fellows? Slow down, please. I need to know what you are so upset about. Please tell me calmly."

"Max puts his no-good books in the way of our freedom and says 'ah ha!' and then goes in the sleeping room for hours and days and leaves us trapped in our small space! We did not do any bad things to those no-good books. The end."

"WORST OF TIMES! WORST OF TIMES! MAX IS FIRED! I DID NOT DO MY POTTY ON THE BAD BOOKS!"

Wally was quiet for a while. "Ah," he finally said. "Now, why do you suppose Max would do a thing like that? I don't suppose you fellows did *anything* at all to warrant such action."

"We did nothing bad or wrong! We were much friendly with the Sophie, who is smart and pretty and good! Max was the thing of jealous. It is not our fault if she thinks he is no good and likes Teddy and Pip much better."

"Ah, the lady caller stopped by, then?"

"We are much liking the Sophie. But Max is acting no good and he is fired. Wally, it is not working out. Not a bit. Please come home!"

"WALLY, TIMES ARE WORST. COME HOME, PLEASE!" Pip said, shoving Teddy so he could put his whole face into the phone. *"MAX IS LYING ABOUT WHAT HE SAYS WE DID TO THOSE BOOKS!"*

"Boys," Wally said gently, "perhaps the two of you need to reflect a while on the events since I left and try to change the way things are going with him by changing your own behavior."

"NO GOOD!" Pip squealed. *"MAX IS BEING NO GOOD, NOT US GUINEA PIGS! HE NEEDS TO CHANGE THE THINGS! HE NEEDS TO BE FIRED!"*

"Wally, friend, surely we are doing no wrong. Max is not working out. We are some miserable. He is doing it all wrong. We need you. Please come home to us," Teddy said.

Wally sighed deeply. "My dear fellows, I am in the midst of a situation here, as you well know, and Amelia is not due for another day and a half...."

"SITUATIONS ARE NO GOOD!"

"Please hang in there for me. I will speak to Max again and ensure that you are getting what you need. You cannot expect him to know what you want and need as well as I do, or Amelia, or Molly. It isn't fair to have those expectations, boys."

"*It is some fair to expect him to not be no good,*" Teddy grumbled.

"Yes indeed, it is. However, your idea of 'good' tends to be a bit different from most individuals' ideas. I will speak to Max. Please remember, no talking when Max is around. Okay, boys?"

"*Do not worry, Wally Best Friend. We have no wanting to be talking to that no-good human,*" Teddy said quietly.

"*WALLY, TELL MAX TO BE GOOD!!*" Pip squealed.

Max picked up the phone when he came back in, sending the guinea pigs skittering away. "Professor, you still there?"

"Yes, indeed, Max. So... is everything going all right? Truly? Are the boys behaving for you? You can tell me."

Max glanced at his chewed-up text books, felt a ripple of guilt wash over him about the ramp-blocking episode, then replied, "Everything's fine. They're great. They just like to make some noise sometimes. Blowing off steam, I guess. But we're good, Professor. Don't worry about a thing. And, uh, the neighbor dude kind of, uh, mowed your lawn. Sorry."

Wally sighed. "Ah. Well, that's that then. If you are certain that there is nothing you would like to share... I will call again tomorrow. Have a pleasant night, Max."

Max stepped up to the ramp. "Okay, dudes. Let's have a truce for real. A truce means we stop fighting. Can we please stop fighting? I'll go get your dinner ready now. You can eat and then take really, really long naps. We don't need to have any more shenanigans, okey dokey? I'll even read you a book if you really want. Give me some sign that that's what you want otherwise I'll assume that you don't. I can easily turn on the TV instead. Do you want me to turn on the TV instead?"

The guinea pigs peeked out of the house and stared silently at him.

Max went into the kitchen to prepare the vegetables.

"WHAT IS THE NEW PLAN?" Pip whispered. *"WE NEED A PLAN! MAX IS STILL HERE AND WALLY DID NOT SAY TO US THAT HE IS COMING BACK!"*

"Pip, there will be no plan happening now. We will not make Max mad again until he has given us our dinner," Teddy said firmly. *"After that time... I do not know yet. I need to do some of my best thinking."*

Chapter Fourteen
Saturday Night

Max found it ironic that all of the quiet was coming at him when he didn't need to sleep. Since they had finished their dinner, the guinea pigs had not made a peep or a mess. He felt suspicious - like, waiting for the other shoe to drop and stuff - but decided that it made sense to take advantage of the silence and do some studying.

But, of course, what he needed to study was Western Civilization. And that book, thanks to the fuzzballs, was history. Max enjoyed a laugh about that clever play on words, then thought some more about his dilemma. He needed a new copy of the book - now.

He called his roommate, Alex, who probably wasn't planning on studying tonight.

"Dude."

"Dude! Where're you?"

"House-sitting. I left a note."

"Huh."

"Need a favor."

"Busy."

"Dude!"

"Date."

"Who?"

"Sara."

"Who?"

"From English."

"Dude...."

"What?"

"Need a book."

"Which?"

"Western Civ."

"Where's yours?"

"Uh... chewed up dude."

"Chewed up? Dog?"

"Guinea pigs."

"Huh? No way!"

"Way. Loaner?"

"Sure, no sweat. I'll leave it on your bed."

"Dude."

"Dude."

"Later."

"Yup."

There was no sign of fuzzballs anywhere. No sound, no sight. Smell? Well, yeah, a little bit. He wrinkled his nose. It was his Econ book that smelled. "Thanks, dudes," he said. "Thanks a lot." He threw the ruined text books into the garbage under the kitchen sink. He would need to take out the garbage before Mrs. Professor got home. He would rather not explain to people who probably loved and respected books just how his got into a position where guinea pigs could do their business all over them.

Max approached the guinea pig house with keys in hand. "Okay, you guys, I need to run over to my dorm room for a while. I need to get a new book for studying 'cuz you two wrecked mine. It's toast, completely unreadable, and, like, smells bad too. So thanks a lot for that. You cost me, like, twenty bucks."

Pip whispered, *"TOAST."* He listened for the sound of the door closing, then said it again. *"TOAST! TEE HEE! THE BOOK IS TOAST, DUDE! ROGER IS TOAST AND THE BOOK OF MAX IS TOAST! TOAST IS A CRUNCHY FOOD!"*

Teddy stopped trying to sleep and wandered over to where Pip was busy tee hee-ing and surely getting ready for singing. *"Pip, you need to stop the jokes and tricks and do some resting."*

"PIP DON'T DO TIRED, DUDE! TIRED IS TOAST!"

Teddy shook his head slowly back and forth. *"Do some tired, Pip. Give it a try this one time. There is much to do this night when Max is back."*

"MAX IS NO GOOD AND WE NEED TO FIRE HIM!"

"Pip, surely we will fire him. That is what we have been working on so very hard all this day and other days. Surely you are not so crazy that you don't know that thing."

"TOAST," Pip said in a little puff.

"Pip, pay attention! It is the time of resting, not the time of saying 'toast'."

"*TOAST IS MUCH FUN TO SAY!*" Pip sang. "*TEE HEE! TOAST IS CRUNCHY BREAD - YOU CAN PUT ON YOUR HEAD! MAX HAS A BOOK OF TOAST - AND PIP LIKES TO BE A GHOST!*"

"*Crazy Pip.*" Teddy went back to his cozy cushion to have a nap, but Pip was already singing a new song.

Max is no good.
He does it all wrong.
He has toasty books,
And can't sing a song.
Pip will save the day
For the pretty and smart Sophie.
Then best friends will come home and we will... eat toast!

Chapter Fifteen
Spilled Beans

Max stepped into the little house with the borrowed text book in his hand, braced for whatever would be. He had calmed himself way down after the crazy events of the day, which was a good thing. Because whatever would be would be, and there was no point in being worked up about it.

He expected noise and mess. It was good to expect that. If he expected that, he would not be surprised or disappointed when he found it. Expect the worst and deal. How he was going to deal was to go to that bedroom upstairs where there was privacy, quiet, and a door. There, he would study and get some sleep. Then, after a shower and putting on clean clothes (wrinkle-free, thanks to Aunt Jane), he would be ready for the big date with Sophie on Sunday.

It seemed like a foolproof plan, like he couldn't lose. That made Max feel relatively cheerful, considering the fact that he needed to study his brains out all night.

But as he entered the house, expecting noise and mess, he got the opposite. This was what he wanted, but not what he expected. Instead of being glad about getting what he wanted, Max was uneasy. He walked suspiciously toward the living room, eyes narrowed. As far as he could tell, there was no new mess in place. Which was, again, what he wanted, but not what he expected. What were they up to?

He turned toward the stairs. Didn't matter. He needed to study, then sleep. They could do whatever they needed to until morning. He just didn't care.

"Pssst!"

"PSSST!"

Max stopped and stood completely still.

"TEE HEE!"

"Shh!"

Okay, that time, the hissing sound was also a... giggle. Max frowned. That giggle was totally creepy for some reason. He shuddered, gave himself a shake, wiggled fingers in his ears, and said, "I do not believe in ghosts. No way!"

"Boooo!"

"I don't believe in ghosts," Max repeated.

"Ooooooo!"

"Not listening!" Max put a sneakered foot down on the first step, which made a surprising creaking sound and made him jump. "It's a squeaky step. There are no ghosts and this is not a haunted house." He stopped, swallowed, looked behind him. "I am going upstairs to study," he said to the ghost-free house. "And then I am going to get a good night's sleep."

But just as his foot touched the step, the telephone rang. The timing was so perfect - or horrible - that it startled him into dropping Alex's book. The book landed in a bit of a heap and in his rush to grab the phone, Max kicked and sent it skidding across the living room carpet and toward the TV.

On top of the TV was that fragile, girlie doodad. It was, once again, in danger of destruction!

Max Grantburg, who was not exactly cut out for baseball but had done his share of time in the outfield, dove for the toppling umbrella-girl artifact - and made the most spectacular catch of his life.

And naturally, no one was around to see it.

Or so he thought.

Teddy and Pip had seen it, and from the guinea pig house came a quiet squeaky impressed little, *"DUDE!"*

Max sat up, massaging his elbow and inspecting the statue. It appeared to be in good shape and he felt relief wash over him. All was well - except the phone was apparently not going to let up. These guys did not have an answering machine. Standing with some difficulty, still gripping the statue, Max grabbed at it and gasped, "Hello?"

"Hello. Is this... Max?"

"Who is *this*?" Max asked suspiciously, not recognizing the female voice as belonging to Aunt Jane, Molly, or Sophie.

"This," said the female, her voice stiffening, "is Amelia Dearling."

Max cringed, cleared his throat, and said, "Hey! How's it going Mrs.... uh... Ms....uh...."

"Amelia," she said.

"Amelia," Max repeated. "What's... up?"

"That is my question for you, Max. I phoned earlier and there was no answer. I became concerned. Is everything all right?"

Max felt unfairly busted. He hadn't done anything wrong! He had just saved her statue! Her guinea pigs had chewed up and peed on his books!

"Max?"

"Everything is *great*," Max said. "I just had to go out for a while. To go get a book. From my roommate. Alex. Western Civ. I have a test Monday."

Amelia Dearling said, "I see," but sounded like she disapproved.

"I have it now - the book - so... all is well. All is great."

"The boys are fine?"

"Yep. Fine. I was just going to, like, read to them like they like so much. When the phone rang, I was on my way to do that."

Amelia's tone got friendlier. "Lovely! They are so enjoying *Harry Potter*, aren't they?"

Max cleared his throat. "Yeah. And me too. We were, like, reading for... hours... earlier. Today. And last night, too. It's... enjoyable."

"How wonderful! You must be nearly finished, then!"

Nearly finished. Hmm. Max made a mental note to move the bookmark to the end of the story – and to ask Molly what the story was all about in case he was quizzed about it on Monday.

"Well, I won't keep you. It sounds as if you and the boys are having a lovely time, and I really do not want to get in the way of your studies. I apologize for sounding... suspicious before, Max. Truly."

"All right. Thanks. I mean, it's okay. It's fine."

"Max? Would you indulge me by placing the phone within the boys' reach so I can speak to them? I know it seems to be a strange request, but it soothes them to hear my voice...."

"It doesn't sound strange to me. Not today. I do that for the professor too. They seem to totally like it."

"Thank you so much. And thank you for understanding."

The totally out-of-sight guinea pigs thumped their way to the phone the instant Max set it down for them. It was as if they had some kind of e.s.p. in their heads. Weird. He could hear Amelia talking at them and the guinea pigs making soft sounds and crowding against the phone.

Max realized that he was still clutching the umbrella-girl statue - his greatest catch and save ever, witnessed by no one. He needed to put it somewhere safe, somewhere the guinea pigs could not get at it with their fruit and whatnot. He chose the little dresser in the guest room. He tucked it against the mirror.

The idea to move the other breakables out of that room and onto the dresser came to him in a flash of brilliance. Why risk more incidents? He might not be able to make an amazing save the next time. His mind on that plan, Max stepped into the living room, not prepared in any way for what he overheard.

A-ME-lia,
A-ME-lia,
Oh, how I love A-ME-lia
Mom Jane is no good.
Is Wally no good?
Oh, how I love A-ME-lia!

Max grabbed onto the door frame.
The little guinea pig... was *singing.*
He wiggled fingers in his ears again and rubbed his eyes.

A-ME-lia,
A-ME-lia,
Oh, how I love A-ME-lia.

Molly is good,
Max is no good,
Oh, how I love A-ME-lia!

Max inched closer as Teddy gave the singing Pip a push and... talked into the phone. Not squeaked or wheeked. Talked. *"Amelia, it is worst of times here with no best friends, only Max who does it all wrong and will not go away. You need to come home now and save our day! Molly Jane is in a place full of monsters. Wally is far away too, and you are farthest. It is no good. We are concerned. We are distressed!"*

Max stumbled back a step, his heart hammering. A ghost haunting the house was one thing, but *this*? This was... another thing. He didn't want to, but looked back at the guinea pigs.

Teddy noticed him, and clearly said, *"Uh oh."*

And the little one said, *"TOAST!"*

Chapter Sixteen
Blackmail

The house went silent except for Amelia's voice saying, "Boys? Boys, are you there?" This was another dream, right? It had to be. And yet, it did not have any of the usual features of a dream. Like being asleep, for example. Max made his possibly sleep-walking way to the couch and slumped onto it. He suddenly desperately needed to be sitting down. The little song kept running through his head: *A-ME-lia, A-ME-lia, oh, how I love A-ME-lia!* He gave himself a shake and put his hands over his ears. "Guinea pigs do not talk," Max said out loud. "Or sing! Especially not sing!" He said it again. Then again. Then again. "Guinea pigs do not talk!"

He needed fresh air, that was all. Lack of fresh air sometimes made a person... hear guinea pigs talk. Fresh air would cure this. He stepped outside. Yeah, that was it. The cool evening air hit him and he felt instantly more sane. There was that neighbor, puttering around in the yard. Normal. Some kids were playing catch in the street. Normal. Nothing but normal stuff going on. He walked to the mailbox, opened it up, and checked for mail. He had already gotten the mail, but checking mail was normal. Max stuck his hand in the box. There was something in there he had missed before: a postcard. Max looked at the picture of a field of tulips, red and yellow, swaying in the breeze. It was addressed to "Teddy and Pip."

Amelia had written a postcard to her guinea pigs.

Not normal.

Max looked back at the house. Something bizarro was going on here. Somehow, anything his cousin Molly was involved in was, or turned, bizarro. He did not have time for this. He needed to be studying now. He sort of had a date tomorrow - with *Sophie*! He had waited nine months to have a date like this and needed to get himself ready for it. He did not need or want to be wondering about ghosts and talking animals right now. Or being insane.

And yet, that's what he was doing: wondering about ghosts and talking animals... and being insane.

But probably it was just a lack of fresh air. And maybe the way he landed on his elbow when he caught the doodad, that amazing catch that no one got to see. That had knocked something loose in his... brain... somehow. The part of his brain that heard animals talk.

Max closed the mailbox and walked slowly toward the house, giving the nosy neighbor a friendly, normal wave. Then he sat on the front step, enjoying more air as his mind started working on the situation inside.

There were two options. Well, no. There were three. The third, as always, was that this whole thing was a great big misunderstanding. A mis-hearing or... something like that. The guinea pigs had not actually talked. He had heard it wrong.

A-ME-lia, A-ME-lia, oh, how I love A-ME-lia!

And yet....

Option 1: Max Grantburg was crazy. He was seeing things and hearing things. In spite of his lack of it, his imagination was creating quite impossible things, and had been ever since he got to this possibly haunted house.

Option 2: The professor's guinea pigs actually *could* talk. And/or there was a ghost. Or the guinea pigs who could talk were making ghostly sounds to freak him out. Because those two could not only talk, but had devious, plotting, scheming minds to go along with it. Possibly, the guinea pigs had been tormenting him on purpose ever since he stepped into the house.

Back to Option 1: Max Grantburg was crazy.

Well, that just figured. He finally had a date with Sophie. Sophie thought he was *nice*. She wanted to see him again. And he had to turn out to be crazy.

A-ME-lia, A-ME-lia, oh, how I love A-ME-lia!

Okay, back to Option 2. Would it be so bad if those guinea pigs could actually talk? Would that reality be so terrible to accept?

Yes.

Max put his head in his hands. He was crazy. What did a crazy person do about being crazy?

He had no idea.

"*It is all right, Pip. We will not do any more talk and Max will forget and go on with his no-good business. But that was a very close one for us indeed!*"

"*IT WAS CLOSE! WE WERE ALMOST CRUNCHY-CRUNCH TOAST!*"

"*From now on we will need to be most sneaky and careful.*"

"*MOST SNEAKY AND CAREFUL!*"

"*If that Max figures out the true truth that guinea pigs can all talk human talk, then we are in great danger, just like the Sophie! We will be put in white coats and doing research in the place of D.C., and that is the worst of all times!*"

"*I DO NOT WANT TO DO RESEARCH!*"

"*The lucky thing, Pip, is that Max is not so very smart, so....*" The guinea pigs turned their little heads slowly until their eyes met Max's. "*... So he does not believe it and will never say a word to anyone,*" Teddy finished.

Pip said, "*CRUNCH!*"

Max pointed to Teddy. He moved his finger from Teddy to Pip, then back again, then back and forth again - and again. "Hold on now. I *heard* you. I heard what you just said, both of you. I heard it. For real. For sure," he squeaked.

"*Whoop whoop?*"

"Uh uh," Max said, shaking his head, his shaky finger still pointing and moving from guinea pig to guinea pig. "I heard you dudes. I am not crazy. I heard it. I heard *talking*. From you two. And I am not crazy!"

"YES, YOU ARE TOO CRAZY!" Pip squealed, then crouched down to cover a tiny mouth with tiny paws. *"OOPS! TOAST!"*

"Ah ha!" Max pointed at Pip, then repeated, "Ah ha!"

"'Ah ha' and pointing is bad manners!" Teddy said.

"Ah *ha!*" Max turned his pointing finger on Teddy.

"WE ARE CRUNCHY, CRUSTY TOAST!" Pip squealed. *"MAX KNOWS THE BIGGEST SECRET AND WILL BE CALLING THE NEWSPAPER NOW! DUDE! DUDE!"*

Max continued pointing and watching, his head shaking fast. "You can talk," he said, his voice only squeaking a little bit now. "I heard it from both of you. You both did it. You talked. I am not crazy. This... is crazy. This is a bizarro situation here, but I am not crazy."

Teddy did a soft sigh.

"You made the noises in the night! You screamed when I was on the phone! On purpose!" Max continued, the finger continuing to point at one, then the other of the guinea pigs.

Teddy and Pip exchanged a look and a shrug.

"You made all of that *mess* on purpose, too, didn't you?"

"Pointing is bad manners," Teddy said again. *"DO NOT POINT THAT FINGER AT ME!"*

Max stood, breathing hard and pointing for a really long time. None of them spoke a word. Then the questions bubbled up too much in his brain and he had to ask: "Why? Why do you talking guinea pig dudes, like, have it in for me? What did I ever do?"

The guinea pigs looked at each other, then back at Max, and Teddy said conversationally, *"We don't like you."*

Pip, shrugging, calmly said, *"WE DON'T."* He looked at Teddy, shook his head some more, then repeated, *"WE DON'T."* The guinea pigs looked at each other again and seemed to shrug. *"THE END."*

"You can't talk. How can you *talk*? That isn't possible," Max demanded. "It isn't normal!"

"MAX IS CALLING US NOT NORMAL!" Pip squealed.

"Of course I am! This is the most not normal thing *ever!*"

"Of course it is normal," Teddy said patiently. *"Max, all guinea pigs can do the human talk. Most do not want to. It is some work, and much, much more easy to only squeal and wheek and whoop. Pip and me have best friends who want to talk. So we talk. The end."*

"I don't believe you!"

"Believing or not is not important to us," Teddy said matter-of-factly. *"The truth is the truth, and we know it and you know it."*

Max frowned, shook himself, and said, "What?"

"If you are not believing, then that is best for us anyway," Teddy said.

"What are you talking about?" Max narrowed his eyes and lowered his voice.

"*If you are not believing, then you are not going to do the bad thing of turning us in to the government for researching jobs in D.C. We do not want to do that thing!*"

"Turning you into – what?" Max rubbed his forehead.

"*WE WANT TO WATCH TV AND LISTEN TO POTTER! RESEARCH IS NO GOOD!*"

"I didn't say anything about...."

"*It is what you will do. You will call the newspaper and bad people will come and our life will be falling to pieces. But you do not believe in this talking, so it is better. The end. Max, go do your studies now. Bye bye.*"

"*THE END! GOODBYE!*"

"Uh... uh...." Max clutched at his head. "This is not normal."

"*Max, it is all right if you need to fall down or get some water. We understand this routine by now. Mom Jane needed a long sit down and some days and days to be all right with our talking. Molly Jane Fisher did that falling down thing and drinking water. Then she believed and saved our day and is a best friend.*"

"My aunt knows about... this?"

"*MOM JANE IS NO GOOD! SHE PUT US IN A BUCKET! DO NOT SPEAK OF HER TO US!*"

"Huh?"

"*Max, we do not want you to be a friend, but we need for you to do no telling of this slip-up to our*

Wally or Amelia. They do not want us to spill the beans we just spilled to you. Or anyone. Else. And a promise is a promise."

"So Molly knows, and Jane...."

"AND DAD! DO NOT FORGET ABOUT HIM! HE IS A FRIEND WHO BRINGS CHRISTMAS!"

"My uncle, too?" Max whispered. "And nobody told me?"

"Of course nobody told you! It is the biggest secret of all times and you are not a best friend or to be trusted!" Teddy said with a shrug.

"Well, uh, I mean...."

"We do not want trouble from you, Max, and so we are going to do the thing of blackmail to you now. Okay?"

Max's mouth dropped open. "Huh?"

Teddy did another sigh. *"Blackmail is a thing humans do to each other to stop bad things from happening to themselves. Plus usually there is money involved, but we do not have that stuff. But we know of Judge Judy, Max, so do not make us mad. Are you ready to hear our demands?"*

Max gave his head a little shake.

"We will not tell our best friends Wally and Amelia about the not reading Potter, no TV, the bad blocking of our walking path with your no-good, smelly college books, your saying of bad things, not believing that we are good, and on and on. That is our deal for you. Your deal is that you will not tell that we did talking in front of you. Plus, you will get our Wally on the telephone and make him come home

- now. Thank you. You can call him right now. We will wait and be quiet."

Max stared at the guinea pig.

"Go make the call! This is blackmail, Max! Do not make us more mad or the mail will be even blacker!"

"MAKE THE CALL!!!!" Pip squealed.

Max narrowed his eyes and crossed his arms. Max Grantburg did not get blackmailed by guinea pigs. He was a lot of things, but he was not a dude that sort of thing happened to. "You can say whatever you want to the professor. He won't believe you. No way. He will believe me. So no deal."

"NO!" Pip squealed. *"DO NOT SAY THAT THING! OF COURSE THERE IS A DEAL!"*

"They will believe best friends, not a stranger called Max who does it all wrong!"

"Even if they do believe you, so what? What do you think they're going to do about it? Ask me to leave? Ask for the money back?" Max smiled triumphantly.

The guinea pigs exchanged a glance and Pip said, *"UH OH. THE BLACKMAIL IS NOT WORKING OUT, TEDDY, I DON'T THINK. WE ARE BEING TOASTED BY THIS DUDE!"*

"How about this?" Max said, stepping closer and crouching so he could be eye-to-eye with the blackmailers. "I *won't* tell the professor or Amelia that you talked in front of me - *or* that you tossed hay and food all over the place, almost breaking Amelia's valuable doodads – *or* that you played tricks on me constantly ever since I got here, pretending to be ghosts and stuff. And in return, you will keep it quiet around here from now on. No more shenanigans. Then maybe I'll keep on feeding you. How's that for blackmail?"

"We want our best friend Wally back!" Teddy squeaked.

"MAX IS DOING BLACKMAIL TO US!" Pip threw in. *"NO GOOD! FOUL PLAY! OBJECTION!"*

"Yeah, see? How do *you* like it?"

"We do not like it!"

"WORST OF TIMES!"

"I am actually holding all the cards here, little dudes. You got nothing."

"MAX IS HOLDING ALL OF THE BAD CARDS AND DOING BLACKMAIL!" Pip shrieked. *"THIS IS A NO-GOOD TURN OF EVENTS!"*

"Call our Wally right now and tell him you cannot do the job anymore. Get him back or else!" Teddy stood up on his hind legs, his face very close to Max.

"Or else?" Max found himself laughing. "Or else what, little dude? The professor is all the way in Minnesota, like, teaching college. It's a big deal and he has to stay there for a week."

"Call Amelia! Call Molly Jane! Call Dad! Call the police!" Teddy started to thump down the walkway. *"Call the Governor! Call Elton John! Summon Harry Potter!"*

"MAX IS FIRED!" Pip contributed, and he thumped off after Teddy. *"EXPELLIARMUS!"* he called over his shoulder.

"Dudes, give up. I win. You got nothing on me. I have all the cards, and you know it."

"*WE DO NOT WANT TO PLAY CARDS WITH YOU, MAX! YOU ARE FIRED! GO AWAY!*"

Max stood for a moment staring after the upset little critters whose little tiny mouths had been spewing out... words and sentences. Unhappy words and sentences. Which was amazing and incredible - and unbelievable. Not normal. He felt a little dizzy, to be honest. It was one thing to argue with four-legged little.... But when he let himself really think on it.... Oh boy. He needed to sit down.

The silence made the guinea pigs stop ranting and thumping. They looked at him. "*Go ahead and fall over, Max,*" Teddy said, his head moving from side to side. "*We will go back to the talk of cards and blackmail when you are done. Get water, too. That is helpful to freaked-out humans.*"

Max sank back onto the couch. He rubbed his face, looked at the guinea pigs again, then rubbed his face some more. He took a deep breath, then another, then let it out very slowly.

"*FREAKED... OUT,*" Pip whispered. "*TOAST!*"

"*Pip knows how to use a celery phone, if you need to have ambulance service,*" Teddy said helpfully.

Max shook his head for a long time, but it did not make the situation go away. Those guinea pigs stayed where they were, talking to him. Giving him suggestions on how to handle the shock of them talking. It was like an oxymoron or a circular reasoning or something. It was bizarro. He needed some water. He finally stood and wobbled his way into the kitchen. He gave himself ten minutes to reflect, absorb, deal, and recover. "Not normal," he said quietly. "But possibly this is what it is. Try to be calm, Max."

"Okay, little dudes, you want your people back. I get that. I'm a stranger and you prefer to have *not* strangers around. I get that, but I can't bring them back right now, not reasonably."

"*DO IT NOT REASONABLY!*"

"We all want something, right? So let's find a way to negotiate. Okay?"

"*We do not negotiate!*"

"*WHAT IS NEGOTIATE?! WE DO NOT DO THAT THING! WHAT IS IT?!*"

"I happen to believe that we can get along, for a couple days, with no fuss or trouble."

"*OBJECTION!*"

"*I think you are not right in your head, Max, if you believe that,*" Teddy said. "*Our deal is for you to get our Wally back. Or Amelia, Molly Jane, or Dad. Now or sooner! Get going!*"

"The professor and Amelia are calling, like, regular. I will make sure you can talk to them as much as you want. Okay? I can't bring them home early, but I can do that. That is what negotiating is."

"*NO DEAL!*"

"*Sorry, Max, no deal. A couple days is too many days. It is days and days and too many of them. The end. Start making calls. We don't like you. The end.*"

"Dudes, I have the cards, remember?"

"STOP SAYING THAT THING!"

"We, too, have cards, Max!"

"WE DO? I MEAN WE DO! SO THERE! MAKE THE CALL!"

"You don't want the professor to know that you talked in front of me, right? You want me to keep on getting food to you, filling your water, and so on and so on? You want me to read a book to you?" Max crossed his arms.

Teddy stood on his back legs. *"You do not want us to do tricks and jokes on you when the Sophie comes here tomorrow, do you Max? You do not want us to make you look like a no-good weirdo stalker in front of the pretty smart Sophie, right Max?"*

He narrowed his eyes.

"Do you?" Teddy countered.

"You don't want to try me."

"Max, you do not want to try us!"

"I'll take Sophie away from here – we'll study at the coffee shop by the mall."

"NO GOOD! YOU ARE CHEATING ON THE BLACKMAIL!"

"You guys have no cards to play. You are one trick or joke away from an informative phone call to the professor. I'm sorry, but he is going to believe me over you. So I win. The end."

"THE END IS OUR THING TO SAY! YOU CANNOT SAY IT! TEDDY, TELL HIM THAT WE HAVE CARDS TOO, AND OUR CARDS ARE THE BEST CARDS! WHY ARE YOU NOT TELLING HIM

ABOUT OUR CARDS?! OUR CARDS ARE BETTER THAN HIS CARDS!"

"Are you ready to talk about a compromise?" Max asked with a smile, and though Pip's head wagged back and forth in denial, Teddy sighed and said,

"Yes."

Chapter Seventeen
The Negotiating Table

"No more sudden shrieking or screaming," Max said, "especially when I'm on the phone. I am a dude who likes and needs food, sometimes food that I call up on the phone, okay? And also, especially no screaming when I am talking to Sophie."

Teddy nodded silently while Pip shook his little head. *"WE LIKE SOPHIE! LEAVE HER ALONE!"*

"And no shenanigans when she comes over. You can have..." Max looked at his watch and narrowed his eyes, "... five minutes with her, then I want you to disappear into that house of yours and stay quiet. Stay quiet and out of sight."

"Max, that is not reasonable!" Teddy squeaked. *"We like the Sophie!"*

Max held up a finger. "Furthermore, there will be no ghostly noises in the night, no hay dropped over that ledge, no wasting water, no destruction of my property, and so on."

"'So on' is not an acceptable legal term," Teddy pointed out. *"Objection!"*

"SUSTAINED!"

"Okay, scratch that."

"SCRATCHED!"

"Behave like guinea pigs, be quiet at night, don't make a mess, and don't mess things up with Sophie. In return, I will not tell the professor that you have been difficult and destructive little talking guinea pigs for the past two days."

"YOU ARE FIRED!"

"Max? I am thinking that we can possibly accept these terms. We would like to have our lawyer present, but we do not have one, so... okay. Pip?"

"OBJECTION! I DO NOT ACCEPT THIS!"

"Pip, we have few choices or none. Max has the cards."

"MAX'S IDEAS SOUND LIKE NO FUN AND WORST OF TIMES FOR TWO DAYS! OUR LIFE WILL BE NO FUN AND MUCH SADNESS AND MISSING OUR BEST FRIENDS! WE WILL BE ONLY SAD AND BORED AND... SAD. We will have no good times and will be in a big depression. Pip don't do... sad. But Pip is... going to be... sad." The little voice trailed off pitifully and the once-spunky little guinea pig put his head down on his paws and went silent.

"It is all right, Pip. Yes, it will be the worst of times, but Max will, at least, feed us. We will not be going hungry. We will, yes, be sad, very sad; and very bored, yes, indeed. But not starving. We can do a lot of sleeping, for days and days... and days and days... and days. So many sad, boring days full of sadness and boredom...."

"Oh, come on!" Max groaned. "No fair! That is emotional blackmail. That is even worse than the other kind."

"Yes, Max, it is badder and blacker, but that is all we have to work with," Teddy said quietly with a little shrug.

Max groaned again as his victory evaporated on him. It was one thing to hold all the cards and another to feel like a big bully about it. "Come on, dudes, it won't be sad. It'll just be normal."

"Normal is not what makes us happy. Max, you do not know how to do it right. You will make us sad. We are sure of it. We are sad already. Look at our faces."

Pip said nothing but his little face sure did look sad.

"We could read together. Would you like that? Will that make you happier?"

"You do not know how to read to us the way we like it," Teddy sighed. *"It will only make us more sad when you do it all wrong. You will probably say the name and scare us out of our little heads."*

"Say... what?" Max gave himself a little shake. "Look, guys, all I really need and want - am begging for here - is some quiet time tonight because I need to impress Sophie tomorrow. I need to study, and I need sleep. If things go well with my date tomorrow – and that is the big, important 'if' - I am at your service. I will read to you, watch TV with you, or whatever you want. Except," he added quickly, holding up a finger, "calling someone to come home early from a trip to replace me. Can we make a deal like that? Help me to impress this girl I like and I will make the rest of our time here together as fun as a dude like me can manage. I might not be a lawyer, but it seems like a pretty decent deal to me."

"We need to talk about this in private," Teddy said, then he and Pip disappeared for a while into their house.

"Max, we will make sure the Sophie leaves this house with liking of you. It will be very hard but will be for sure. Pip and me have some skills about making human match-ups, though we do not like to do that thing too many times. We will do this for you as part of the deal. We will let you have the night for sleeping and will help you to study for your big date, though studying for dates does not make sense to us. Dating is watching TV and eating food and is best when all friends are together. But if you are sure that there is study to do, we will help with it. We help Molly Jane with her studies lots of times and are very good with it."

"WE ARE ROCK STARS AND DON'T YOU FORGET IT!"

"Thank you," Max said, suppressing a smile. "That sounds awesome."

"Then, because of this most reasonable help, you will owe us as much reading as we can take. But never say the name. Then you must play Harry Potter with us and be the bad guy. Then there must be music listening time - Beatles White Album. And then...."

"Dude, don't get carried away, now, okay?"

"And then," Teddy continued, *"Pip would like to have lessons on how to talk like a dude. The end. Those are our demands. Now, get your book about Western Whatever and we will start to explain it to you and also help you with your vocabulary sentences."*

"How to talk like a dude, huh?"

"PIP WILL WRITE A SONG IN THE NEW DUDE LANGUAGE AND IT WILL BE A BIG HIT!"

"Okay, cool."

"PIP IS A ROCK STAR!"

"So you said."

"I WILL SING TO YOU MY BEST SONGS! THERE ARE MANY, IT WILL TAKE SOME TIME AND THEN SOME MORE TIME! AND YOU BETTER LISTEN!"

"So you two are going to make sure Sophie leaves here liking me, huh? How?"

"That is for us to know and you to find out," Teddy said. *"Come on, Max, let's get going on the homework."*

"What caused the ultimate failure of the western portion of the Roman Empire?" Max asked.

The guinea pigs stared. Pip scratched his ear.

"Well? You said you'd help. What's the answer, dudes?"

Pip said, *"OBJECTION!"* and wandered away.

"I am guessing that this part of the empire you speak of was no good and that is why there was the failure. To me, it sounds like Star Wars somewhat." Teddy nodded confidently.

Pip returned and said, *"WE DO NOT LIKE VADER! HE IS FIRED! DO NOT SPEAK OF HIM!"*

"Thanks for that, Teddy. And I'll keep that in mind about Vader, Pipster. Now, I need to take this book to that room, close the door and bury my nose in it for, like, ever. Or until tomorrow morning. I'll see ya then, okay?"

Chapter Eighteen
Being Smooth With the Ladies

It was late Sunday morning. Max was clean, his clothes were clean, and the little house was clean. This time he was not wearing pajamas and had no hay in his hair. The guinea pigs were fed. The soggy bedding under their water bottle had been replaced with fresh stuff, and everything smelly was now outside in the garbage can. Max had honestly never done so much manual labor on a Sunday morning in his life. Facts and figures from centuries past floated around in his brain as he approached the guinea pigs for the third time.

"WRONG!"

"That is still not the right way to dress for a date, Max! Try again!"

Try again? He was already dressed in the best he had: a plaid shirt (clean and smooth), a pair of jeans, clean socks, and his sneakers. The guinea pigs had rejected the last two shirts, sending him back to the guest room with loud protests.

"Dudes, this is all I've got. I'm tapped out."

"Max, we are giving the advice we know about how to have a best of times time with the Sophie," Teddy said. *"The way to dress is in a suit, tie, and white shirt. Shoes must be shined and hair must be... better. You are also not wearing the cologne or a flower on your suit like I told you. You are not listening well! Try again!"*

"YEAH, DUDE!"

"Look, you little fashion-policemen, I am a nineteen-year-old college dude. I have no suit and I only wear a white shirt for, like, deadly serious times when my mom makes me. So don't even go there with me. A tie? Uh uh. My shoes can't be shiny 'cuz they're made of, like, cloth. If I wear cologne, it'll send a wrong message, I think. And no way am I putting a flower anywhere on me."

"Max, you are taking the wrong attitude and pathway," Teddy said, shaking his head.

"IF YOU DO NOT LISTEN TO US, YOU WILL NOT HAVE A GOOD DATE! THE SOPHIE WILL FIRE YOU RIGHT AWAY AND THAT WILL BE THE END!"

"Look, guys, I am what I am. I can't, like, dress up as your best buddy Wally. I just don't roll that way. Okay? If Sophie doesn't like me because I don't dress very good - I mean, very *well* - then I guess we aren't meant to be. But she seemed to like me yesterday even though I was, like, a total mess. Thanks to you guys."

The guinea pigs were silent for a while, then Teddy said, *"But Wally is the thing of smooth with the ladies, Max. He is charming and smooth and knows what to wear. Amelia is liking of him very much."*

"WALLY IS BEST OF TIMES! YOU ARE DOING IT ALL WRONG!"

"Let's move on. I am not changing my clothes again. No way."

The guinea pigs shook their heads at him. *"Stubborn and not-cooperating is also not going to make this a good date,"* Teddy said. *"The lady is right and has the say. She is the boss, and you need to say this, 'Yes, dear, you are right.' Plus also and always be ready to say, 'Sorry, my dear, for I was wrong.'"*

Max smiled and shook his head. He actually had no response to that.

"Giving flowers to a lady is a good thing. Roses are best, but be careful for the prickly stems."

"ROSES ARE SCARY SCRATCHY THINGS!"

"Dudes, seriously? This is a study date. Giving her flowers would seem... pushy and not appropriate. Trust me on this one."

"It is a good thing for the man to do fancy cooking," Teddy went on as if Max had not spoken. *"Ladies like that thing very much. It is because then they know that the husband in the marriage will do the cooking sometimes or all the time. Ladies do not want to be always doing the cooking. Only when they feel like it."*

"Dude, I'm not, like, trying to get married here. Don't make me totally break out in a sweat." Max rubbed the back of his neck nervously.

"SMELLY SWEATING IS NOT GOOD FOR DATING! DO NOT DO IT!"

"Exactly. Let's not go there."

"*MAX, WE WILL NOT GO ANYWHERE! YOU NEED TO STAY HERE SO WE CAN HELP YOU!*"

"That was just a figure of speech, Pip dude."

"*DO NOT DO FIGURES OF SPEECH AT ME ANYMORE! THEY ARE NO GOOD AND SOME CONFUSING!*"

"Roger that."

"*Max, it is best not to speak to Pip of Roger.*"

"Huh?"

"*DO NOT SAY THAT NAME!*"

"Uh... okay. Got it."

"*Now, back to the cooking,*" Teddy said.

"Dude...." Max groaned.

"*What can you make if you are no good at fancy cooking?*"

"Nothing."

"*WRONG ANSWER!*"

"*There is something. Think harder!*"

"I could probably heat up a frozen pizza...."

"*Pizza is not the thing of romantic! 'Heat-up' is not cooking!*"

"*OBJECTION!*"

"I can make a sandwich...."

"*NO!*"

"*Sandwich is even less cooking. Max, there needs to be more if you want the Sophie to be impressed over you. Pizza and sandwich sounds like dude stuff. Sophie is not a dude and please do not say to her the word of 'dude' or she will do the silent treatment at you, I think. Be careful with that stuff!*"

"DO NOT CALL HER 'DUDE'!" Pip squeaked. *"DUDE IS A NAME FOR BOYS AND NOT THE SOPHIE!"*

"Got it. Good advice."

"Tell her nice things about herself, like her prettiness and smartness. Ladies like to hear that thing."

"Also good advice. I'll try."

"Do not talk to her like she is a dude. She is not a dude. She is the pretty and smart Sophie who you want to turn into your wife."

Max coughed. "Dudes, seriously."

"When she is your wife, we will give you new tips and ideas and rules. The rules are much different then."

"Okay. I'll be sure to stop by in a million years when that happens."

"Max, a million years is too long to be waiting for a wedding. It is best to do the elope or Sophie will turn into Bridezilla, and we know all about that bad thing. Pip might not be able to save your day for you, so watch out. You can have your wedding at Molly Jane's house on Christmas Eve and we will agree to wear our black hats if you ask nicely. Honeymoon is too scary, so do not do that part, okay?"

"Dude, I just want to get through the afternoon. You're making me, like, sweat with your talk of weddings." Max rubbed at his neck.

"Do not be sweaty when you are around the Sophie! Ladies do not like sweaty and smelly boys. P.U.!"

"Yeah, well, you guys are making me sweaty. It's not my fault."

"GO TAKE A SHOWER SO YOU DON'T STINK!"

Max looked nervously at his watch.

"Max, the important thing is to not be no good," Teddy said seriously. *"Do not say things that are a lie, do not do the exaggerate, do not say mean things about people or pretend you know everything when you don't know anything. Honest is good. Ladies do not like lying or bragging."*

"BE POLITE!"

"Now back to the big problem of fancy cooking...."

"Maybe we should order in."

"Order in is better than dude-food, that is for sure."

"TEE HEE! DUDE-FOOD SOUNDS MUCH FUNNY AND I WILL WRITE ABOUT IT IN MY NEWEST HIT SINGLE!"

"Speaking of this topic, singing or guitar-playing is a good romantic way to be, Max. Ladies like it very much. And also poetry-reading. Pip can help you when you are ready for that. Do you know how to play the guitar, Max?"

"Dude, seriously? No. Not at all."

"Dude, yes. I am quite, quite serious."

"Is the professor a guitar player?" Max sighed.

"No, Max, our Wally does not do that thing. But he is smooth in all other things and can say right things and also smell good, so he does not need it. He can do the poetry with the greatest of ease for

Amelia. Since you have none of his smooth skills, you must play the guitar for the Sophie. Do not fret, Pip will help you with musical things."

"PIP IS A ROCK STAR AND MY SONGS ARE POEMS ALSO IF THEY ARE SAID AND NOT SUNG! I WILL LEND YOU SOME WORDS! DO NOT GET THEM WRONG!"

"Guys, I am not a singing dude. Or a poetry-reading dude."

"Max, what kind of dude are you, then?" Teddy asked, standing up against the railing and studying him. *"You are not good at clothes or hair, cooking or romantic stuff...."*

"I don't *know*. That's the problem. I just plain... don't know." Max sat on the couch. "Maybe nothing."

Pip said, *"UH OH!"* and Teddy thumped his way down the walkway until he was close to Max again.

"Do not do the thing of giving up, Max. Not when we have wasted so much time on you so far."

"All I can tell you is... I like her. That's all. I can't give you a reason why she would like me back. Except she likes you two."

"OF COURSE SHE IS LIKING US! WE ARE ROCK STARS!"

"Max, surely there is some one thing that you can do. Surely. Every human has one something they are good at. I hate to say this thing, but even Mom Jane is good at things."

"WRONG! MOM JANE IS NO GOOD!"

"Yeah, my aunt is great at lots of stuff - cooking and laundry and being a mom...."

"She does not smell bad and has done a good job of being Molly Jane's mother. And I bet there are other things she does well. Dad seems to like her pretty much."

"BAD BARBARA IS NOT GOOD AT THINGS! SCARY EVELYN IS NO GOOD!"

"Pip the point of this talk is not to speak of those two ladies who tried to ruin our perfect lives. The point is to talk of what in the world Max could be good at, because it seems like there is nothing to work with here."

"COME ON, MAX! GIVE US SOMETHING TO WORK WITH!" Pip squealed.

Max wracked his brain for a while. "Dudes, it's like I am totally average in every way. I can do stuff, but none of it, like, really good. Or *well*."

"Average sounds like a no-good thing to be," Teddy mused. *"Average means most people are the same as you. That is not something to be shooting for, Max. Think of something that you are good at. Think hard, and then think harder. I cannot do this part for you. Until not very long ago I was quite sure that you were no good at all, so I am not the one to be asking. Pip either."*

"THINK MAX! COME ON DUDE, YOU CAN DO IT!"

Max shrugged. "I... have a cool car."

"Having a cool car is not something you are good at," Teddy said, scratching his head. *"It is a thing you have. That is not the same thing."*

"But I take care of it and it always runs, like, perfectly."

Teddy said, *"Hmmm,"* and scratched his head some more. *"Maybe. Maybe that is something to work with. But I am thinking that ladies are not caring so much about cool cars. Ladies are more caring about the cooking and laundry. Plus also they do not want to ever take out the garbage and do not want to have to tell you to do that thing. They do not want to talk about garbage, or touch it, or smell it or have it on their minds ever. Garbage is P.U. and they want their man to be in charge of it completely. Can you handle that, Max?"*

Max stared at Teddy for a while, then said, "Dude. This is a study date. I don't think there will be much garbage involved. As long as you two keep the shenanigans to a minimum."

"Max did a good job of cleaning up this most excellent house today," Teddy pointed out. *"It is fresh and clean and we are not unhappy about anything for the moment. That is something. For us to be happy with a human who is not a best friend is saying something. Pip, am I right?"*

"I AM HAPPY FOR THE MOMENT, DUDE!"

"So... maybe I'm not so terrible at taking care of you guys, meeting all of your demands and so on."

"You are also the thing of humble," Teddy said thoughtfully. *"Humble is a good human thing, I think. It is the opposite of bragging and boasting, and ladies prefer it. Good job. Being no good at anything but not pretending you are is something. Confusing, but true."*

"Yeah, I got humility in the bag, I think."

The three were quiet for a while, reflecting on humility.

"Now there is the matter of your hair being all wrong."

"What? I combed it!" Max smoothed at his hair.

"COMB IT AGAIN! AND BRUSH YOUR TEETH!"

"You dudes are, like, harder on me than my mom ever was."

"Max, if you want to be smooth with the ladies, messy hair, joke T-shirts, not-brushed teeth, and wrong words will surely not work for you. We are doing our part to help you, and your part now is to listen. Okay? Comb... your... hair."

Max retrieved his comb from the dresser of the little guest room and worked it through his hair again.

"Now we will practice saying the right words," Teddy said. *"Do not listen to Pip about this part or you will make the Sophie much afraid or too much laughing."*

"DO NOT SAY THAT THING! PIP KNOWS THE RIGHT WORDS FOR TALKING TO PRETTY, SMART SOPHIE!"

"Firstly," Teddy said, *"you will call her the name of 'sweetheart,' 'darling,' or 'my love.' That is smooth, and ladies like it very much."*

"No way!"

"If you call her a name of 'hey you' or 'hey' or 'dude,' you will get the thing of silent treatment surely. Or possibly doors will slam in your face."

"Dude, Sophie and I are, like, still getting to know each other. We are not ready for... that stuff. I need to call her Sophie, and that's about it."

"'Sweetheart,' 'darling,' or 'my love,'" Teddy insisted.

"DO NOT CALL HER 'HEY YOU'!"

"You must find out what her favorite music is and play that stuff while you dance with her, but do not step on her feet or she will think you are the thing called clumsy."

"We aren't dancing today, dude. We're studying."

"Dancing is better when the music is not Beatles or disco. Try Sinatra or big band."

"Noted. Okay, dudes, I need to figure out what to do about lunch."

"Just do not have pizza or sandwich! Pizza will make her mad! Sandwich is boring dude-food!"

"How in the world do you know things like this?"

"TV, Max. You should watch TV too. Then you would know this stuff! Plus also we are watching our Wally, who is much smooth with Amelia. Amelia is much liking of him, and loving."

"Yeah, well, they're also, you know, married. And stuff. And older and wiser."

"Do not tell Sophie that she is old! Do not ever say that thing! Do not ever say to her that she looks fat!"

"Dude! Do you think I'm an idiot?"

"Max, that is not a question to ask if you do not want to hear the answer."

"Okay. Back to lunch."

"Ladies like to eat salad and drink iced tea."

"Salad?" Max frowned. "Like, give her some of your stuff?"

"DO NOT DO THAT THING!" Pip squealed. *"PIZZA IS FINE! DO NOT LISTEN TO TEDDY ABOUT THIS PART!"*

"Would it make her hate me if we ordered some Chinese?"

"The Sophie is not a Chinese person," Teddy pointed out. *"I am thinking that she will not want that stuff."*

"All right, never mind about food. I will wait until she gets here and let her decide."

"Max, that is a smart idea and a good one. Ladies like to be the boss and tell you what to do. Good job!"

Max felt surprisingly proud of himself and grinned. "What else?"

"What else is now we are going to do a test run of your date. Are you ready? You are going to be Max. I will be the judge and Pip will be the Sophie. Ready?"

"OBJECTION! I AM NOT A GIRL!"

"Pip, it is called acting, and rock stars do it all the time. You are being the Sophie and please do not be the thing of ridiculous about it. Thank you. Ready?"

"Dudes, I can't do this."

"Ding dong! That is the doorbell, Max! Go get it and say hello to your pretty and smart date! Remember: 'sweetheart,' 'darling,' or 'my love.'"

Pip thumped his way to the end of the walkway so he would be next to the door.

"Open the door, Max!" Teddy ordered.

Max opened the door, feeling ridiculous. "Hi Sophie," he mumbled.

"'Sweetheart,' 'darling,' or 'my love'!" Teddy squealed.

"HELLO MAX. YOU ARE NOT WEARING A SUIT TODAY AND SO I AM NOT IMPRESSED!"

"Dude, seriously?"

"DO NOT CALL ME DUDE! SING ME A SONG AND IT BETTER BE A GOOD ONE OR I AM LEAVING! WHERE ARE MY FLOWERS? I WANT A SALAD!"

"Sorry, Pip. This is not working out. You are fired as the Sophie."

Chapter Nineteen
Sophie

When the doorbell rang - for real and not pretend - Max felt like he had forgotten everything. Every fact and figure from the late-night study session about Western Civilization, and all of the stuff the talking guinea pigs had been schooling him on all morning. It was all gone, leaving him with a completely empty head. Not a good situation.

Max wracked his brain and tried to remember a few of the guinea pigs' better tips. *Do not call her dude. Tell her she's pretty. Let her decide what to order for lunch....* He opened the door.

"Hi, Max," Sophie said with a smile.

That smile left him not only empty-headed, but speechless too. "Uh...." Max stepped back so she could enter. "Hi," he finally choked out.

Sophie was wearing jeans and this... blue shirt. And there was that hair... those eyes... and that smile. "Are you ready?" she asked.

"For...?" Max felt himself break out in ridiculous sweat over that simple question. Of course he wasn't ready. He was far, far from ready. How could she know? Was it that obvious?

She smiled and tilted her head a little. "For studying?"

He cleared his throat and tried to look smarter. "Yes. I am ready for studying. Let's study."

Teddy groaned softly. *"He is not doing the smooth, Pip! Not in any way! We maybe have wasted our time!"*

"IS IT THE TIME FOR A PLAN B? CAN WE MAKE A MESS NOW?!"

"No, Pip, I think we will give him some more time to turn this around. Be quiet now and remember: no talking. We have spilled enough beans already. Shhh! Maybe Max can find a way to be smooth after he gets done with some bumps."

"Where are Teddy and Pip?" Sophie looked around.

"Don't worry, they'll be out," Max said. But would they? They had not actually discussed how those two would work into this study date. He had said last night that he wanted them out of sight and quiet. Would they take that seriously? Even though now he totally wanted them to come out?

"Where should we sit? Kitchen table? The couch?" Sophie asked.

Max gestured toward the couch after a slight panic, and Sophie sat. She pulled her notebook out of her backpack, flipped through some pages, then smiled up at Max.

"I like your shirt," Max blurted.

Sophie glanced down at it. "Oh. Thank you," she mumbled, looking embarrassed. "Um... yours is nice too."

"I don't have a white one here. Today. Otherwise...."

Sophie tilted her head a little.

"Do you want to talk about lunch? You can decide what we eat. We'll order something in." Again he blurted and sounded ridiculous.

Sophie set her notebook down slowly. "Oh. Okay. Um...."

"If you want a salad, we can do that. No problem. Whatever you want. And I'll take care of cleaning up. Totally. Cleaning up is what I do. You don't have to think about or touch any garbage at all today. Or ever when you're with me."

Sophie tilted her head at him again.

"How about music? I can put on some music! What do you like?"

"Music? Aren't we going to study?"

"Oh. Right. Never mind. We'll just be studying. Quietly. No music."

"Max? Are you all right?" Sophie narrowed her eyes, still smiling, but not as much now.

"Yes. I am." Max sat on the edge of the couch and fumbled with his text book. His cell phone started ringing from the guest bedroom and he jumped up immediately, knocking the text book to the floor. "That's my phone!" he said too loudly and sounding too happy about it. "I need to get it. I'll be right back."

Then he dashed from the room, closing the guest room door behind him.

He stood against the door, breathing hard, then snatched up the phone. "Hello? Aunt Jane?"

"No, Max, it's me - Molly. What is wrong with you? Why are you breathing funny like that?"

"Oh. Hey, Mol. Everything's fine here. I gotta go."

"Gotta *go*? You just picked up! You can't hang up on me. I need to know what's going on! I'm calling you all the way from Florida, you know!"

"Look, Molly, I have company right now, so I gotta go."

"Company *again*?" Molly's tone made Max feel ridiculously guilty.

"It's fine. Nothing for you to get all freaked about. Furthermore, it is a girl I need to impress and so far I am failing at that, like, spectacularly. So... goodbye."

"You have a *girl* there?! Mom! Max has a girl there!" she called without covering the mouthpiece first.

"It's okay! The professor knows all about it. I mean her. We're studying. It's a study date, and it's cool. Except it isn't because I'm, like, sweating."

Molly giggled.

"And it isn't even the slightest bit funny."

"Sorry, Max. I can't even imagine *you* with a girl."

"Thanks. That is very nice of you to say. All right, ask your questions. I'll give you one minute, then I gotta go. Starting... now." Max was not kidding about the one minute. He watched the second hand on his watch.

"How are Teddy and Pip?"

"Awesome. Nothing to talk about there. Smooth as silk. We're getting along like best buds."

"What? Really? Not really. I don't believe you."

"Yes, really. It's true. What else do you want to know?"

"Lie. How are they for real?"

"Don't argue with me. It's true. What else do you want to know? You have forty seconds."

"How was Tweets when you fed him this morning?"

Max froze. He had forgotten all about Molly's bird. Darn it! He smacked himself on the forehead.

"Max? How is Tweets? Why aren't you telling me how he is?"

"He is fine! Nothing is wrong with anyone. I just need to get back out there and study. Okay? I have been away too long and...."

"Did you give Tweets a treat this morning like I told you to? He gets sad when I'm away, so he deserves something extra. Please tell me you didn't forget!"

Max squeezed his eyes shut. "Molly, I didn't forget anything. All is well. Go have a fun time on the Dumbo ride or whatever."

"We're at *Epcot* today," Molly said. "We are in a really long line to see a show, and Mom and Dad are getting grouchy about it."

"Yeah, well, long lines are a bummer. I gotta go, kid."

"Geez, Max. All right, fine. Say hi to Teddy and Pip for me. Don't neglect them so you can make googly eyes at some *girl*. That is not what you are being paid for."

Max had a very strong urge to say, "Yes, dear." Instead, he said, "I know. I am going to go check on them right now. Okay? I'll tell them hi for you, and give them some extra eats. Okay?"

When he returned to the living room, Sophie was peering into the guinea pig house and calling softly to Teddy and Pip. "Where are they?" she asked, sounding disappointed. "Yesterday they were so friendly."

Max cleared his throat. "Uh... guys? Come on out and say hello to Sophie, okay? Remember Sophie and how much you liked her yesterday? Come on out. Please. I would appreciate that. I also would like to see you. Very much. The professor and Amelia would really like for you to be friendly instead of hiding out. Coming out and saying hello is good manners."

Nothing happened. Max gave Sophie a little smile and a shrug.

"Is everything all right?" she asked. "Was the phone call an emergency?"

"Oh! The phone call. No. My cousin Molly. She's ten. She's at Disney World. In line to see a show at Epcot. No emergency. She just wanted to talk. The line was long."

Sophie smiled about that. "How sweet. Does she call you often?"

"Uh. Yeah. Often." Max raised his eyebrows. "I'm feeding her parakeet this weekend, in addition to watching these dudes. I, uh, need to go give the bird his breakfast, I guess. I was studying so much that I didn't get around to the bird-feeding. *Yet.* I should do that. Sorry. I'm really sorry about that. It'll be quick. I promise."

Sophie's eyes got wider and she said, "Oh. You have to... leave? Now?"

"Sorry. But they live just down this street." He pointed in that direction. "It's just a short walk. An even shorter drive. I could drive there in fifteen seconds, probably. Or less."

"Well...." Sophie fiddled with her notebook. "I could come along. If you wouldn't mind."

"You could? I mean you *could.* Sure you could. We could go together. Walk to the Fisher's house. To feed the bird. Sure." He was sweating again. Dang. "Would you *like* to do that?" Max ran a hand over his forehead.

"Yes, I would." Sophie set her notebook down and stood up.

"Really? I mean... okay. Great. Let's go. I just need to get the key. To lock up and then to unlock at the other house." Max ran his hand over his hair. "If you're sure."

Sophie smiled. "I just need to use the bathroom first. If that's all right."

Bathroom... bathroom... was the bathroom clean? Was it tidy? Did it... smell all right? "Yes. Of course," Max croaked. "Go ahead." *Please let the bathroom be tidy and not smell bad!*

He crossed his fingers about that, then paced his way up to the guinea pigs' house. "Guys? What are you *doing*? You're leaving me high and dry here! Come on out and do your cute stuff for her! She wants to see you and I am so totally bombing! I thought you were going to help me here! Remember our little blackmail agreement and arrangement? Huh?"

Nothing. Not a squeak. Sophie was coming out of the bathroom already.

"So... I'll be right back little dudes," he said, turning up the volume. "Don't freak out. I'll lock up and stuff. I just need to go feed that bird I told you about. Then I'll be right back and I'll give you guys a little treat. Okay? When I get back we can hang out. Okay? We'll hang out together. All of us. Together. That would be totally okay with me. Never mind what I said last night about that. Okay?"

He got no response from Teddy or Pip, but Sophie was smiling at him.

Max wiped at his forehead. "They get, you know, nervous when they're alone too much." He cleared his throat, jingled keys, then said, "Shall we go?"

The day was warm and a soft breeze blew as they walked along the sidewalk. Sophie commented on houses and flowers and the nice day and Max babbled back, trying to say the right things, but probably not accomplishing it. She was so pretty.

"Here we are. This is my cousin's house." Max turned the key in the lock and was hugely pleased when it opened. He stepped inside and immediately heard a ruckus.

The ruckus made Sophie giggle. "Sounds like somebody's hungry! What's the bird's name?" she wanted to know.

"Uh...." Max drew a big blank. A really big one. What the *heck* was the bird's name? He knew it. He did. Molly had just mentioned it on the phone. What the heck *was* it? "Polly," he blurted, which was so stupid, because he was sure the bird was a him. He recovered quickly. "P-a-u-l-i-e," he spelled for her. "He's upstairs. In a cage. Do you want to... come upstairs with me? You don't have to. But you can. If you want. He's in Molly's room. He's really noisy, so you don't have to."

"I'd love to." Sophie smiled. "I love this house!" she said as they climbed the stairs. "It's so cozy!"

"Yeah, it's... something, this house." Max cleared his throat. It suddenly felt *too* cozy and too warm in there. "Hey, Paulie!" he called as he stepped into Molly's room. "Take it easy, dude! We're here to take care of all your needs. So chill. Stop freaking out."

Sophie giggled about that and looked around Molly's room. "What a cute room!"

"Hmm, cute," Max mumbled, fumbling with the bird cage door. "Molly is a cute little kid, that's for sure."

"She's ten? Is that what you said?"

"Uh huh, ten," Max said, still fumbling with the door.

"Hi Paulie!" Sophie said, stepping up to the cage and peering at the green and yellow, head-bobbing, screeching creature. "You are a pretty bird, Paulie!"

"*SCREEEEEECH!*"

"Heh heh. Yeah. He's noisy. Animals just love to make noise around me. Shhh!" he said to the bird, then reached in to grab the seed cup. And in a flutter of wings and happy whistling, the bird flew out. He flew right out of Molly's room and on to who knew where.

Max stood frozen with the seed cup tilting so stuff spilled onto the floor.

"Oh my gosh!" Sophie breathed, then covered her mouth to stifle giggles. "Oh, Max! Where do you think he went?"

Max closed his eyes for a second, then forced himself to unfreeze. "He'll be back," he said, forcing confidence. "No biggie. I'll get him back in." Feeling sweaty again, he went about the business of filling the food and water. He added some of the treats to the top of the seeds and asked himself why everything had to go wrong.

"So, it's all right that he's out like that?" Sophie giggled.

"Sure. He does that, like, all the time. No big deal. He likes to get out and... stretch his little wings. You know. He's cooped up, like, all day and...." Max stifled a sigh. How in the wide, wide world was he going to get that thing back in the cage? Molly had not given him any instructions except about feeding the thing. She had actually said it'd be best not to let him out because he might be hard to get back in.

"Do you want me to start looking for him?" Sophie offered. "In case he doesn't come back right away?"

"Oh, no. I can do it. Like I said, he does this all the time. He'll be back."

"I don't mind. Let's both look for him. It'll be fun!"

"Well... be careful, because...." Max looked at Sophie's pretty hair. "He sometimes...." He patted the top of his head.

"What?" Sophie tilted hers.

"Well, sometimes he lands on... a person's head." Max cringed.

Sophie laughed.

He spotted a sparkly beret hanging over the post of Molly's bed, grabbed it and handed it to Sophie. "Wear this. Just in case."

Sophie found the idea of wearing Molly's sparkly hat to be delightful and funny. She put the hat on her head with a giggle, peered at herself in Molly's mirror, wrinkled her nose, and asked, "How do I look?"

"Beautiful," Max heard himself say. He waited tensely for fallout.

But Sophie only smiled and murmured, "Thanks." Then she left the bedroom to go in search of that danged bird whose name was definitely not Paulie. What in the world was the actual name? Something goofy, like, not a real name. It was... something. Oh, whatever. At least it wouldn't be able to turn him in or blackmail him about this. Or would he? It would just be his luck that the bird was able to talk too. It would actually make more sense than the talking guinea pigs did. A talking bird was, like, common and normal. So the bird could probably talk and would rat him out to Molly, or was ratting him out right now to Sophie. Otherwise there would be a bizarro discussion and more blackmail to deal with next time he stopped by to feed the thing. Geez. He could not get a break. And why were Teddy and Pip not helping him out today like they said they would? They said they would make him look good, make sure Sophie left actually liking him. All he knew for sure was that she was getting a good laugh over this date. And those double-crossing guinea pigs were not helping one bit.

The search for "Paulie" took about fifteen minutes - fifteen minutes that should have been spent studying or talking about lunch.

Sophie found the bird on a blade of the ceiling fan in the kitchen.

"Oh, Max! There he is! Hi Paulie! Come on down, sweetie!" Sophie held out an optimistic finger with a big smile. "Come to Sophie!"

"Watch out - he might... you know. He might bite you."

"No, he looks like a sweetheart, not a biter," Sophie insisted. "Come on down, Paulie!"

This time, the bird obeyed. He made a dive and landed - not on Sophie's offered finger, but on Max's head. And Sophie was delighted. She covered her mouth to stifle giggles.

"He... does that," Max said. "All the time. He likes to be up high. You know. No big deal."

Sophie was stifling her laughter so hard that tears were forming in her pretty eyes. "I'm sorry, Max. It's just so adorable! Here, duck down so I can get him off for you," she insisted. "Come on, Paulie. Sit on my finger, okay? Come on, sweetie!"

Max could feel his hair being tugged either by feet or the beak, then heard Sophie suck in her breath. "Uh oh," she breathed. "Oh, Max, oh no! It's – uh oh. He just...."

"What?!"

"Paulie left you a little present. In your hair. Sorry!" She burst into giggles. "I'll get it. Just hold on. It's not that bad."

"Are you saying that bird just pooped in my hair?"

"It isn't... big. It's just a little thing." Sophie giggled some more and was sorry some more. She grabbed a tissue from a nearby box and took care of it. "I got it all, so don't worry."

Max sank into a chair feeling absolutely and completely horrified.

"You can wait here if you want. I'll get him back in. Come on, Paulie! You have yummy treats upstairs!"

Sophie, the girl of his dreams, was taking care of the bird for him while he slumped at the table, being sweaty. The bird had *pooped on his head*! The bird whose name he had forgotten and had forgotten to feed.

Just when he thought he had hit the bottom of the barrel, Max heard the sound of vacuuming. Sophie was also cleaning up Molly's room for him. He put his head in his hands.

Sophie appeared a couple minutes later, smiling and hatless. "I found a little hand-held vacuum plugged into the hallway outlet. I got that pile of seeds cleaned up," she told him cheerfully.

"Thanks," Max said as his stomach did a growl loud enough for the neighbors to hear.

"Oh my gosh!" Sophie exclaimed. "Let's have lunch right away when we get back. I'll make us something."

"*No!* I mean, no thanks. I'm taking care of it."

"I don't mind."

"No. I want to. I'm sorry about all this," Max mumbled, smoothing very tentatively at his hair as they walked toward the door. "What a mess."

"Sorry? Why? That was *fun*," Sophie insisted.

"Yeah. Right." Max locked the door. "Let's go see what fun is going on at the other house, okay?"

Chapter Twenty
A Promise is a Promise,
and a Deal is a Deal

"They're still not coming out," Sophie remarked, looking disappointed.

Max cleared his throat. "Yeah. Weird, huh?"

"I thought they liked me."

"They do like you. A lot," Max said. "It's, like, their nap time, that's all. They were, like, up late partying last night. Right, little dudes? So what about lunch?"

"What do you feel like eating?" Sophie asked. "You must be starving, based on that growling I heard."

"Oh, that was... yeah, I'm hungry. I admit it. But you get to choose. We'll order in."

"Anything is fine. What's close by?"

"Uh... no idea. Do you want a salad?"

Sophie tilted her head at him and raised her eyebrows. "No thanks. How about pizza?"

"No!"

"No?" Her eyes went wide with surprise.

"We don't have to have pizza. We can have what *you* want."

"I think I want... pizza," Sophie said slowly.

"Are you sure? Really sure? Really, really sure?"

"I think so."

"Because I'll get whatever you want. Anything. If you honestly do want pizza, it's yours. No problem. I'll call a pizza place. But don't choose that just because...."

"Max? Are you okay?"

"Yes. What kind of pizza do you like?"

They got their notes out while waiting for the delivery guy to show up, and Max offered her iced tea.

"No thanks. Do you have a Coke?" Sophie asked.

"Well, yeah, but if you want iced tea...."

"I would actually love a Coke."

"Okay, but iced tea is a definite option," Max said, though he wasn't sure there was any in the house.

"Coke would be great," Sophie said, tilting her head at him. "Please?"

While he poured her a glass over ice, half of which had gone rolling all over the kitchen floor, the quizzing began. And Max's brain, which had emptied of all facts and figures, gave him nothing to work with. The bird-poop-on-the-head incident was still bugging him, and he just plain could not come up with any answers. "Sorry," he said when he returned, setting the Coke on the coffee table on top of his notebook. "I didn't hear you so well, what with the ice falling all over the floor." He cleared his throat.

She smiled and handed him her notes. "How about if you quiz me?"

Max was relieved about this and began reading off questions. But his relief changed to feeling stupid when Sophie got every question right. Compared to her, he was the worst student in the whole class, probably.

"Max?" she was tilting her head at him again. "What's the matter?"

He rubbed his empty stomach.

"Yeah. I know. I'm hungry too." She smiled.

"I think better after I eat."

"Me too," she agreed.

"You, like, already know it all," Max said.

"Oh, *no*, not really." Sophie looked at the text book. "I have no idea what to write about for the essay questions. I'm really worried about those."

"Essay questions," Max echoed, cringing. "Me too."

The doorbell interrupted. Then chewing, swallowing, and talking about how good the pizza was saved Max from the topic of the test for a while.

"I sure wish Teddy and Pip would pop out and say hello," Sophie said, again glancing up at the walkway, looking wistful. "Are you sure they're all right?"

Max finished chewing, ran his tongue quickly over his teeth, then lips, then wiped his mouth thoroughly before speaking. "They were fine earlier," he said. "We were hanging out and... talking. You know. They were fine."

"Hmm. I wonder why they're hiding from me today."

"They're not hiding from you. I think they're more likely playing mind games with me."

"No. I'm sure that isn't true." Sophie smiled. "They love you."

Max shook his head. "Trust me, they think I'm one of the dumbest humans alive."

"What? No!"

Max laughed. "No. Trust me."

"I think it's me they don't like." Sophie made a pretty little pouty lip.

"Sophie, they like you. More than me, for sure. I mean they like you more than they like me. Not that I don't like you. Because I do." Max snuck a look at Sophie after saying that awkward thing and found her to be smiling.

"You do?"

"Sure. Of course. Yes. And they do, too. They think you're pretty and smart," he added, and felt himself smiling back at her.

"They do, do they?"

"Yep. They told me."

"They told you, huh?" Sophie wiped her hands on her napkin. "Max...." Her cell phone stopped her from saying whatever she was about to say to him (maybe that she liked him, too? Was that possible?) She looked at the ID and her smile faded away. "Excuse me. I need to take this," she said quietly. Then she stepped into the kitchen.

"Dudes! What in the world is going on with you? You said you'd help me today and you are so not doing that! Come out!" Max hissed, then stuck his head right into the house. The guinea pigs did not seem to be in there. "Come on guys, where are you? Stop playing games! Remember the deal? Remember the negotiating table? I have all the cards, right? Me! Not you dudes! I need your help!"

Max sank onto the couch. "Everything I do or try to do is a disaster. It'll only take her a few more minutes of so-called studying with me to figure out that I don't know anything about the class. Who am I kidding anyway? Max Grantburg is not good enough for a girl like Sophie. I am probably not good enough for, like, anybody."

"Max, do not start the despairing. We have a plan. Be ready to do the right thing. You will know what and when that is. Do not do anything wrong."

Max whipped his head around but did not see Teddy anywhere. "Dude? Where are you? What do you mean by that?"

Sophie stepped back in. She was smiling, but her smile seemed a bit thinner. "Sorry about that," she said.

Max jumped up from the couch. "Let me clean this mess up. You know, take the box out to the garbage and stuff. You just sit tight, okay? We'll study more in a second. If you need to make or take more calls, go right ahead. I don't mind. At all. It's fine." Max took care of the pizza box and moved their glasses to the kitchen.

The guinea pigs had a plan and that made him nervous. This date was already going so badly. Pure weirdness. Whatever they had in mind could only make it weirder, and he did not actually need that.

"Max?" she called. "Is everything all right?"

He was about to answer that when the guinea pigs burst out of hiding and started up a startling tirade of screams, wheeks, whistles, snorts and sirens. This effort put all of their past performances to shame. Max dropped empty Coke cans onto the floor.

"Wheek! Wheek! Wheek! Wheek! Wheek! Wheek! Snort!"

"EEEEEOOOOOEEEEEOOOOO!"

"Wheek! Wheek! Wheek! Wheek! Wheek! Wheek! Snort!"

"EEEEEOOOOOEEEEEOOOOO!"

He stepped into the room. "Dudes, what's up?!" he hollered. "Knock that off! You're, like, freaking out my guest! What's the matter in here? What happened?"

The squealing and sirens continued as he stepped cautiously up to the walkway. Max looked into Teddy's little face, hoping for a clue. Was he imaging it, or was Teddy nodding very slightly as he continued to wheek and snort? He was nodding. Max was sure of it. But what was he nodding about?

Teddy stood up against the railing, looking right at Max. The wheeking turned rather pitiful-sounding, the snorts increased. "*What*, dude? What do you need? Are you hungry? Thirsty? Not feeling right?"

And then Teddy stood a bit higher against the ledge and, somehow Max knew that this was the help. He had no idea what he was supposed to do, or how the noisy outburst could help, but he knew it was the plan.

"Something bugging you, Teddy? You bummed out? Feeling lonesome or upset?" Max asked.

Teddy increased his volume a bit.

"You miss your friends, don't you? You miss the professor and Amelia. And Molly. I get that."

Teddy's pitiful wheeking subsided a bit.

"Okay, little dude. Calm down. You calm down, too, little Pip." He held out a tentative hand and touched Teddy's head. He quieted and pushed himself up against Max's hand. *"Pick me up!"* he said in a very soft voice. *"But do it right or I will bite you! I am not joking, Max!"*

Max picked up the guinea pig, supporting his surprising weight with one hand and continuing the petting with the other. "There," he said. "That's better, right? Just needed a little T.L.C., right buddy?" He couldn't be sure, but it seemed like Teddy was glaring at him. Max continued to stroke his head as Sophie joined him. "There you go, fella. I gotcha. You're okay. Everything is okay. Max is here."

"Oh, how sweet!" she breathed. "Max, that is so sweet!"

Pip continued his siren sounds as Sophie reached out and stroked Teddy's head. "Could I... take him? Do you think he'd be okay with that?"

Teddy snuggled into Max's arms, which made Sophie smile - and Max, too. "Uh... he seems to, you know, not want to move. Very much. Sorry."

"That's okay," Sophie said softly. "I think Pip needs some cuddling too. I'll get him." She reached out to Pip, but he streaked away from her hands, back toward the house, then came streaking back, standing near Max and Teddy while continuing his siren sounds.

"Oh!" Sophie stepped back, surprised. "He wants... you."

"Dude!" Max said, giving Teddy a look. "What's with this? What's with Pip?"

"Pick up Pip now," Teddy said in a tiny voice. *"Put me in the arms of The Sophie. Trust us, Max, we have a plan! Do not mess this up!"*

"Uh, here, take Teddy," Max said, carefully transferring the furry bundle to Sophie, who looked very pleased. "Here you go, Teddy, here's Sophie. She's, like, awesome and will take good care of you while I see what's bugging the Pipster."

Sophie cooed at Teddy and cuddled him in her arms.

"We kinda bonded last night, like, extra," Max explained. "Pip and me are, like, you know, buds now. Right little dude? He's just being particular. For a few seconds. He'll snap out of it."

Pip made a rumbling noise as he was picked up, then settled down and allowed Max to pet him."

"I think it's nice," Sophie said, "how much they like you, Max. That says a lot, I think, about you."

Pip started to chew on Max's shirt.

"Oh! Uh oh!" Sophie giggled.

"Hey, this is my best shirt!" Max said mildly. "Knock that off, Pip-a-roo." He sat down on the couch and Sophie sat beside him. They enjoyed some quiet time, just sitting and petting the guinea pigs nestled in their laps. After a while, Max sensed that Sophie was looking at him. It made him nervous, but also strangely happy. Teddy made his way across Sophie and curled up on Max's lap beside Pip.

"Oh. Sorry about that," Max mumbled. "Whatcha doing there, Teddy?"

"Don't be sorry, Max. It's nice."

"They really do like you. A lot. I *know* it. This is, like, temporary insanity or something."

"It's okay," Sophie said. "I think it's really sweet. I think you are really sweet."

Max continued to pet the guinea pigs, feeling it would be best to keep his mouth shut and let her talk.

"Not just right now, with the guinea pigs," Sophie continued. "All the time."

Max cleared his throat. "Aw, no, I'm just a regular dude. Totally average."

"No. That is not true."

He looked at her. "Well, hanging out with me isn't boring, at least."

"Max, I don't remember when I've laughed so much or had so much fun."

"Really? You're having fun?"

She smiled. "Yes! Can't you tell? Spending time with you the past two days has cheered me up *so much!*"

"Cheered you up?" He frowned a bit. "What was wrong?"

Sophie shook her head. "I've been going through a hard time. It's a lot of things – my roommate, my parents, my ex-boyfriend...."

"Ex... boyfriend?"

She shrugged. "I haven't felt happy or like laughing, for real, in a really long time."

"Well, there's, like, always a lot to laugh about around me."

"It's been nice." She smiled. "Really nice."

"Yeah? Nice?"

"Yeah."

Max smiled. "Really?"

"I can't imagine my old boyfriend being so sweet with guinea pigs, or his cousin's pet bird, or house-sitting. Or anything nice. Or sweet."

"Yeah, well, I like to help out." Max did a humble shrug.

"I would like it if we could spend more time together."

Max said nothing for a long time. In fact, he was struck completely mute until he felt the lightest little bite on his pinkie finger, compliments of Pip. "I would like that, too. Yes. Me too."

"Cool." Sophie smiled. "This is so nice, Max."

"But I don't *live* here, remember? I'm just house-sitting. My dorm room is, like, a disaster. And I have this roommate, Alex, who is... around. And a mess."

"Max, I don't care about that."

"A big mess."

"So we can meet someplace else. There are lots of places on campus where we could sit and talk."

"Without guinea pigs in our laps. These guys do live here." Max gestured to the guinea pigs in his lap.

"Yes, I know. But I still want to meet and talk. I really do."

"Sophie, I want that too. Like, more than anything, but...."

Her face fell a little. "But what?"

"No, no, no! Wait a minute! You are... awesome. I'm the one who.... The truth is, I'm not any good at Western Civ. I barely know this stuff and will probably flunk the test," he blurted.

Sophie's eyebrows went up.

"Sophie, I'm not a smart dude. Not like you are. I mean, you're not a dude - not at all! I meant you are *smart*. And I am *so*... not. Smart. Like you. I'm not as stupid as I might sound right now. Maybe I just haven't found the thing I care about enough to work at it really hard. Definitely not Western Civ. You know? I'm good at computers. And I have a cool car...."

Sophie put a surprising hand on his shoulder. "Max? I like you. You make me feel happy. I want to spend time with you feeling happy. Okay? After today, we don't ever have to talk about Western Civ again."

He had nothing to say about that, so he just smiled.

"Do you want me to help you study for the test?"

"Do you have, like, seventeen hours?"

Sophie laughed. "Not quite, but I do have all afternoon. And there's no place I'd rather be than here with you."

"Wow. I mean, huh. I mean... awesome. Me too."

"Great. So let's get started."

Epilogue

"Max, you do not need to know the details of our perfect plan," Teddy said, his mouth stuffed full of veggies. *"It is top secret and filed away now forever. Be happy that you have another date with the Sophie and be quiet while we munch."*

"BE QUIET! WE ARE EATING!"

"Dudes, I just want to thank you. And I'd like to understand. Okay? Is that so bad?"

"We saved your day and now you owe us! What is there to understand? Pip and me are much good at making the human match-ups. We told you that already."

"NOW WE WILL PLAY POTTER AND YOU WILL READ AND READ TO US! PLUS ALSO YOU WILL TEACH ME TO TALK LIKE A DUDE!"

"I will do all that. I promise. I just want to know how you got the idea to do what you did, 'cuz it worked, like, perfectly! It's freaking me out just a tad that you two are tons smarter than me when it comes to girls."

Teddy finished chewing, then did a little sigh. *"Max, it is much about paying attention and listening. Ladies like to be listened to and paid attention to. Very much. Not just looking at their prettiness, but paying real attention. We did some listening when the Sophie was on her celery phone in the kitchen. She was having a frowny talk in there. We listened hard. It was a talk about not wanting to be together anymore with a person. We are thinking it is a no-good dude who is making her say words like 'insensitive' and such. She says to this person that she is not interested in doing the relationship anymore. She is through. And she is wanting a person to talk and listen, to be sweet, not bragging. We told you this in our talk, Max. Ladies do not like bragging and lying. They prefer humble. They prefer a dude who is not good at anything but does not lie and say he is. That dude is you! The end."*

"She was breaking up with her boyfriend right here in this kitchen?"

"Perhaps. Or perhaps not," Teddy said with a shrug. *"She was talking of wanting sweetness, so we made a plan to make Max look that way. Even though he is a blackmailing bad guy. Tee hee!"*

"Aw, dude. No. Not really. You don't really think that, do you?"

"YOU HAVE ALL THE BAD CARDS!"

"Yeah, but dudes! Aren't we, like, friends, for real now? After all we went through?"

"No. Not really. Tee hee!"

"WE DON'T LIKE YOU!"

"Oh. Well, darn." Max grinned.

"*But you still need to read to us and play Harry Potter with us! Not-friends can do that thing! Tee hee! Right, Max?*"

"*DO NOT SAY THE NAME!*"

"Well, no matter what you say, I say we are friends. For real, dudes."

"*Max, you are a lot of trouble. I am not sure that friends are supposed to be that way.*"

"Hey! You guys are, like, nothing *but* trouble!"

"*PIP IS NOT TROUBLE, PIP IS A ROCK STAR!*"

"*Do not get the idea that you are in the Best Friends Club now, Max! If there is any liking between us we need to keep it secret, like the secret of our talking not being told to you by us. Nobody can be a best friend who does not know about our talking. And you cannot know it or else we will be in big trouble with Wally and Amelia. So... sorry. The end.*"

"This won't be an easy secret to keep," Max said.

"*Max, you must keep it! It is something too important to not keep! Pip and me do not want to do research in DC!*"

"*KEEP THE SECRET!*"

"I will. I totally will. It'll just be... tough. Especially to keep it from Sophie."

"*You cannot tell the Sophie! She will want to tell one friend, and so on and so on and then everyone will know!*"

"*I DO NOT WANT TO DO RESEARCH!*"

"Yeah. I know. I get it. I won't tell. Let's be secret friends, okay? Three dudes with a secret club."

"MAX, WE CAN BE NOT-SECRET FRIENDS FOR ONE MORE DAY, SO LET US GET GOING ON THAT!" Pip squealed.

"Okay, little dudes. Let's get going on it." Max smiled at them, his head shaking. *Bizarro,* he thought, *but in an awesome kind of way.*

"Let's get going with the reading! You lied to our Amelia saying we almost did the thing of finishing the book, so let's now do that thing! Let us fix the lie!"

"Who would've ever imagined me reading a book out loud to guinea pigs? I actually always wondered what that whole *Harry Potter* thing was about." Max picked up the book and opened to where the bookmark was placed. "Now, what's the name I'm not supposed to say?"

"WAIT! STOP! PIP NEEDS TO SING THE NEW HIT SINGLE! SO BE QUIET AND LISTEN! IT IS CALLED A WRAP SONG BECAUSE IT IS LIKE... WRAPPING PAPER. I THINK. LISTEN!"

Being a Dude (A Hit Single)
By Pip

I am a dude.
I eat dude-food.
I do not cry
'Cuz I'm a guy.

I am a dude.
I eat dude-food.
Sometimes I'm rude

But can't be sued.

I am a dude
I eat dude-food.
I do not sing
Or do anything.

I am a dude.
I eat dude-food.
But that's okay
I get girls anyway.

"*Get girls?* Seriously?" Max shook his head.
"*PIP IS A ROCK STAR!*"
"Yeah, little guy. You sure are. Give me paw!"
"*PIP IS GIVING PAW! TEDDY, YOU ARE NOT SEEING THIS! I AM A DUDE NOW!*"
"*Good for you, Crazy Pip. Max – start reading!*"

THE END

PIP'S HIT SINGLES
NO DAY IS GOOD WITH MOM JANE IN IT
No day is good with Mom Jane in it.
Mom Jane puts everyone in buckets.
No day is good with Mom Jane in it.
Mom Jane doesn't like guinea pigs.
No day is good with Mom Jane in it.
But Wally and Amelia don't believe me.
No day is good with Mom Jane in it.
But Pip is me and I saved the day!
The end.

MAX IS NO GOOD
Max is no good.
He does not do what he should.
Max must go
This I know.

Pip is saving the day.
Teddy says o-kay.
Max must go
This I know.

MAX LIKES FOOD
Max likes food.
Max calls Pip a dude.

Max does it wrong.

This is his song.

WE HAVE HAD NO READING TODAY!

Max likes food.

Max calls Pip a dude.

Max does it wrong.

This is his song.

WE HAVE HAD NO TV TONIGHT!

TOAST

TOAST IS MUCH FUN TO SAY!

TEE HEE! TOAST IS CRUNCHY BREAD

YOU CAN PUT ON YOUR HEAD!

MAX HAS A BOOK OF TOAST

AND PIP LIKES TO BE A GHOST!

WE WILL EAT TOAST

Max is no good.

He does it all wrong.

He has toasty books,

And can't sing a song.

Pip will save the day

For the pretty and smart Sophie.

Then best friends will come home and we will... eat

toast!

AMELIA

A-ME-lia,
A-ME-lia,
Oh, how I love A-ME-lia!
Mom Jane is no good.
Is Wally no good?
Oh, how I love A-ME-lia!

A-ME-lia,
A-ME-lia,
Oh, how I love A-ME-lia!
Molly is good,
Max is no good,
Oh, how I love A-ME-lia!

BEING A DUDE

I am a dude.
I eat dude-food.
I do not cry
'Cuz I'm a guy.

I am a dude.
I eat dude-food.
Sometimes I'm rude
But can't be sued.

I am a dude
I eat dude-food.

I do not sing
Or do anything.

I am a dude.
I eat dude-food.
But that's okay
I get chicks anyway.

SPECIAL BONUS
MY SONG ABOUT CORN – by Pip
Corn corn corn corn...
I don't eat that thing called
corn corn corn corn...
I don't know much about
corn corn corn corn.
The end!

For more fun with Teddy and Pip, go to

www.teddyandpip.com

Made in the USA
San Bernardino, CA
13 December 2012